# The Case of the Zodiac Sampler

## A Cozy Mystery

By Beverly Schemmer

Kids At Heart Publishing LLC
PO Box 492
Milton, IN 47357
765-478-5873
www.kidsatheartpublishing.com

© 2017 Beverly Schemmer. All rights reserved.

No part of this book may be reproduced, stored in a retrieval system, or transmitted by any means without the written permission of the author.

First published by Kids At Heart Publishing LLC 2/3/2017
ISBN # 978-1-946171-02-3
Library of Congress Control Number: 2017932156

Printed in the United States of America
Milton, Indiana

This book printed on acid-free paper.

To order more copies of this book go to
www.kidsatheartpublishing.com

*The books at Kids At Heart Publishing feature turn the page technology. No batteries or charging required.*

## *Dedication*

"To the talented and caring ladies of Wanna Bee Quilters from Randolph County, Indiana"

*To Reed & Mary —
Hope you enjoy reading this — It was fun to write —
Best Wishes!
Ben*

## CHAPTER ONE

Belle would have been fine, except she woofed when she spotted Wally Newton across the street about to unlock the door to Wally's Barber Shop and Emporium. Wally heard, then spotted Belle. "Well, good-morning Miss Belle," he yelled and bowed low to her from the waist. At that, Miss Belle took off running across the street dragging her leash behind. A surprised Wally stooped ready to catch Belle. He had assumed her leash was secured.

Virgil Shaffer was approaching the intersection from the north in his shiny black Ford Crestliner in route to the post office. He slammed on the brakes causing him to veer wildly to the left trying to avoid Belle. For a second it was touch and go until Belle emerged from beneath the black behemoth to jump into Wally's arms, her leash dangling. Virgil's sleek shiny car ended atop one of the slush piles on the corner, the nose pointed upward toward the Oak and Main Street signs.

Virgil, with difficulty, slowly opened his slanted door and stepped out into the knee deep gray laced slush. "That dumb dog," he yelled at Wally standing with Belle in his arms. "Can't you control that stupid mutt?"

"She's not my mutt," Wally replied soothing the still frightened Belle. "Are you all right Virgil?"

"I reckon if I can get my car out of this ice pile. Can you give it a push?" he asked surveying his situation.

Across the street, Laura Alice emerged from Sisters' Sewing Shop wearing sunglasses, a maroon wool coat, and a blue plaid headscarf. When she saw the commotion on the corner across the street she yelled, "Are the streets slick, Virgil?"

With the appearance of Laura Alice, Wally put Belle down and she briskly trotted across the street back to her owner her leash once again trailing. Laura Alice quickly grabbed the leash, and picked up her darling pet, "What were you doing over there?" she asked the now yapping Belle who was no doubt telling her owner what she had just been through.

Virgil didn't answer Miss Laura's question about the streets, yet under his breath he repeated, "Dumb dog."

Laura yelled once again, this time asking, "Can I help?"

"No, Miss Laura, we've about got it," Wally replied, as he was now standing in the slush knee deep with Virgil. They gave the car a good shove sending it with a bounce into the street.

Both men brushed the clinging slush that covered their pants from near their knees to their feet. Virgil thanked Wally profusely and Wally gave Virgil a hearty pat on the back as Laura Alice looked on. Virgil at last got into his car and continued on his way. The post office would open a few minutes late today.

"You coming tomorrow night for games?" Laura yelled to Wally.

"Like usual, Miss Laura," Wally responded. "I'm bringing Ralph Stillwell if that's all right," Wally added. "He's bringing dominoes if you ladies don't mind. He's not much of a card player he says."

"That's fine," Laura yelled back, then added, "We'll have applesauce cake."

"You've got a snake?" Wally questioned.

"No-----never mind! See you later," she yelled and waved

before she and Belle took off heading north.

One thing about Wally, although people told him all manner of things in the barber's chair, he didn't always get it straight. He once told Laura Alice that Irma Stillwell, the wife of banker Ralph Stillwell, had died. It wasn't until Laura Alice and her sister, Polly Esther, sent a sympathy card to Ralph that Irma, his wife, stopped by the shop to tell them a thing or two. She had barely been out of sight when the sisters broke out laughing. She dyed all right. Her hair was now as black as it might have been when she was twenty, fifty years ago. Wally obviously hadn't gotten the gist of Ralph's story.

Poor thing, when Irma really did die, last year, Laura Alice and Polly Esther had gone to the viewing. There lay Irma in Waldron Brother's Funeral Home with at least two inches of a snowy white crown above her head and the remainder of her glory a shade of faded black. Ralph stood next to the casket in deepest grief, while his wife, Irma, lay there in deepest humility.

On the way home, each sister promised the other she would never dye her hair. "And sister, if I'm out of my mind and do so, don't let me lie in the casket with my hair like that," Laura Alice pleaded.

"And the same goes for me. I would be so embarrassed, even if I were dead," Polly Esther replied.

So Ralph's coming with Wally on Friday. I hope I don't think about Irma's hair while he's there. Laura thought, smiling to herself. Hmm. . .Ralph's a widower now.

Laura and Belle walked briskly past the B.P.O.E. lodge just north of the sewing shop, past Sampler Club member Ethel Connelly's yellow house, then two empty lots before they came to Virgil Shaffer's house. Everyone who lived in Deerfield knew who lived in each of the houses along Main Street and most knew who lived on the side streets as well.

The twosome stopped at the empty lots before Virgil's house

for Belle's convenience, before heading home. While Laura waited for Belle, she turned to admire the stately dark red two story brick house set deep on the lot just northeast of where she and Belle had stopped. Ralph Stillwell the banker lived there. Even though Laura Alice had been born and raised in Deerfield, that house was like a foreign nation at the edge of town. She didn't know anyone who had ever been inside. Irma Stillwell certainly hadn't been sociable, nor was Ralph. They didn't bother anyone, nor did anyone bother them.

A small grove of walnut trees separated the banker's home from the church and its grounds which included the parking lot. Ralph Stillwell did let the young people from the church collect the walnuts each fall to sell for their youth projects. Wally said it was just to keep the grove cleaned up, but anyway, it was a nice gesture.

Further south along Main Street was Waldron Brothers' Funeral Home run by the last of the Waldron family, Ezra Fritz's mother had been a Waldron. Ezra had never married leaving some doubt about the future of the business which was now in its third generation.

The Deerfield State Bank with an access drive to the parking lot behind occupied the next space. And finally, the last building on the street was Wally's Barber Shop and Emporium directly across the street from Sisters' Sewing Shop owned and operated by Miss Laura Alice and Miss Polly Esther Monroe. The maiden sisters had been born and reared in the same house as their shop.

Further south along Main Street was Miller's Lumberyard, Cox's Grocery, and Ted's Service Station & Quick Lunch. The quick lunch consisted of soup of the day and pie of whatever kind Ted's wife decided to make. The faded sign above the station, still readable, read, 'Eat at Ted's and Get Gas.' Those doing so were mostly the farmers going to and from the Deerfield Elevator and Feed Store next door. Apart from the post office on Oak Street, this was Deerfield. Of course, the county seat, Trenton, was only ten miles away if anyone needed to go to the big city.

The traffic was usual for a Thursday in Deerfield. The bread and milk vans were making deliveries, and a few vehicles were already parked in front of the bank in readiness for it to open. A rusty black pick-up truck with sacks of grain piled in the back rattled along the street going south spewing a cloud of black exhaust. Laura quickly covered her nose with the corner of her scarf while Belle expelled a hearty sneeze. Everything was usual in Deerfield this morning. *Thank goodness nothing much ever happens here*, Laura thought as she made her way home. *There's the war in Korea, but we're safe here. Everything stays the same.*

Inside Sisters' Sewing Shop, Laura was greeted with the sweet, spicy scent of applesauce cake filling the air. Sampler Quilting Club would meet today at 1:00 p.m. Miss Polly Esther, the baking sister, was busy with a customer. Fabric had been measured and cut, now she was helping find the right color of thread at the display. "Hazel's getting ready to make an Easter dress," Polly noted.

"Won't this make up pretty?" Hazel said showing Laura Alice the fabric. "And this pattern is just right." Hazel smiled as Polly held the perfect color of thread to the fabric. "You ladies are always so good to help. Don't you know, Easter is on the 13th this year. At least it's not on a Friday. Of course it wouldn't be. It would be better if Good Friday was on the 13th, but I guess we can't change the calendar."

"Hazel, if you need any help with that dress be sure and let us know. We don't charge any extra for a little advice if it gets tricky," Laura added.

"I almost forgot to show you something," Hazel said opening a small bag she clutched next to her purse. "I got this just this morning at the bank. That new fella, they called him Warren, gave it to me," she stated taking out a thin and narrow box. "It's called a Bavarian Whetstone," she continued while showing the contents. "Warren said it's to advertise the new Power of Attorney services they're offering for senior citizens. It's supposed to remind us that the bank could sharpen our assets. It's supposed to be good for sharpening scissors and knives too."

"Well what do you think of that?" Laura said as she looked over the long oval ended stone with the name Deerfield State Bank stamped on the center. "What did you have to do to get it?"

"I didn't do a thing. I just went in to deposit a check and that Warren fella gave it to me. He's taking Ralph's place you know since he retired. He's related to Ralph, but I'm not sure how. With all the cutting you ladies do around here, I thought you might like to get one," Hazel said before putting her whetstone back in place, writing a check for her goods and leaving the store.

"We should get us a whetstone. That would be good for keeping our scissors sharp," Laura noted. "Maybe I should go on over there before they give them all away. Do we have any checks in the cash register or money to deposit?"

"I reckon we do. Hazel just gave me a check, and I think there are some others. Why don't you go while you've still got your coat on. I'm all set here. We need to check out that new fella anyway. I wonder why he would want to come to our town? Wally said he came here from that bigger bank in Trenton."

Sure enough, Warren was still handing out Bavarian Whetstones along with a smile, a glad handshake, and a pamphlet about the new Power of Attorney service offered by the bank.

*I'm going to tell Polly Esther he reminds me of that huckster at the country fair who sold us that slicing gadget, all smiles and a smooth spiel,* Laura thought as she walked back to the shop looking at her new toy. *I hope that new service works better than that vegetable slicer,* she thought remembering how it had rusted after the first time it was washed.

She caught herself about to cross the street mid-block. In fact, she had stopped off the sidewalk, but stopped short when a car came out from the bank parking lot and turned in front of her. She stepped back then continued to the end of the block, crossing in front of the barber shop instead. She tried not to jay walk, at least not in broad daylight. Town Marshal Homer Collier was likely somewhere about. Sometimes it seemed he was everywhere. He certainly took his job seriously and she wanted to stay on his good side. After all, Homer was the son-in-law of Thelma Goodwin who came to Sampler Club each week. He was married to Thelma's daughter Sue Ellen and the father of Thelma's grandson, Skipper, who delivered their daily paper.

Thelma was as proud as she could be of his position and usually mentioned it in some way during club time, although, it wasn't likely that anyone had forgotten. The ladies let Thelma have her claim to fame as the mother-in-law of the town Marshal. Besides, Thelma had hinted that Homer would someday like to be the country sheriff. Maybe that was just her idea, but who knew?

Nettie's brown Hudson parked in front of the Sister's Sewing Shop at 12:30 p.m. She and Thelma said they wanted to come early to look around at the new fabric before club time. Polly told them about the Bavarian Whetstones and they both left in the Hudson to go to the bank. Vesta and Ethel, the other members of the quilting club, came later and took off by foot for the bank across the street and down half a block. Likely no one would be there for the Sampler Club time at 1:00.

As it turned out, Vesta and Ethel got back at 1:05 followed by Nettie and Thelma at 1:15. It seems Nettie had parked her Hudson in a 'no parking' space in front of the bank and Marshal Collier had given her a warning ticket. Thelma said it was a courtesy since she, his mother-in-law, was in the car. At least that's what she told everyone.

Each club member now had a Bavarian Whetstone and was thrilled with the gift. Since everyone wanted to sharpen scissors before cutting the pieces for the new block, Laura gave a demonstration about using the whetstone. After a few awkward attempts, they were satisfied, and ready to cut. "You'll need to be extra careful with your fabric and your fingers," Laura warned. "Don't try to work as fast as you did before or you're likely to have an accident."

"What do you think of that new fella, Warren?" Ethel finally asked when they were all working. "He seems nice enough to me, not too bad looking either. He has dark wavy hair like my Cecil had when he was young."

"Ralph never gave away anything that I can remember when he was there," Vesta added.

"I wonder who pays for free stuff? Does it come out of our money? It's a bank you know," Thelma inquired.

"Well, they do make money from interest they charge on loans. Maybe it comes from that," Nettie said.

"I don't think they could just take money from our accounts. I'm wondering about that new Power of Attorney thing Warren is advertising. I'm going to check into it after club's over," Ethel added. "I could use some help with finances. Cecil used to take care of all that and since he's gone it's a burden. I'm always afraid I'm doing something wrong. It would be good to have a nice fella like Warren help me."

"It wouldn't hurt to find out about it. I don't know if it

costs something extra or if it's free. I'll give that paper to Karl to see what he thinks," Vesta said.

"I don't think I need that kind of help since my son-in-law is the marshal," Thelma added. "He and Sue Ellen already help out, and they wouldn't let anyone cheat me."

"Say, since Pisces is our new block, does anyone have a Pisces birthday?" Nettie asked. "It's from February 19th to March 20th."

"I do," Ethel responded. "My birthday is March 11th. I reckon I'm a Pisces. I read my horoscope in the paper this morning. It said that there are changes coming and I need to be cautious. I wonder what I'm in for? Whatever, it means, it never hurts to be cautious."

"You're in luck today," Polly added. "I baked an applesauce cake for us to have with tea this afternoon. It can be for your birthday, Ethel, even if it isn't today."

"We should find out what our signs are and have a little treat each month when we're working on that sign," Thelma said. "I don't think anyone had birthdays in January or February, did they?" They looked about at each other, but no one claimed a birthday for those months.

"Does anyone have a birthday for our next sign, Aries, March 21 to April 19th?

How about Taurus, April 20th to May 20th?" Thelma continued to question. "I'll even make the cake. I've got a new recipe from the paper. It's called Dipsey-Doodle Date Cake. Doesn't that sound good? The date part, I mean. I like dates."

"It sounds interesting. I don't know about the 'dipsey-doodle' part. I don't like to admit it, but I have a birthday in May," Vesta said. "I'd rather forget about birthdays anymore."

"Oh, come on now," Laura said. "You might as well celebrate that you're still alive and kickin', and you've got good friends who are glad you are."

The conversations about horoscopes and birthdays died down as the quilters began cutting the pieces for the new block. Finally, Laura Alice interrupted the calm with, "Let's break for cake and tea. I think we've all got off to a good start. Then, if we don't talk too long, we'll have about another hour to work."

"It's nice to have cake or a treat of some kind once a month even if there's not a birthday," Nettie said. "Since Vesta has a birthday coming up, our treat that month can be for her. Thelma, you can make that 'dipsey-doodle date' then."

"I hope I remember," Thelma said. "Maybe you all can help me."

Everyone liked the applesauce cake. It was just right with tea.

After refreshments, the ladies continued with cutting the pieces for the new block until Karl arrived for Vesta. He parked as usual behind Nettie's Hudson in front of the shop. He always tapped on the horn three times to let Vesta know he was there. Somehow that had come to be the signal to the group that Sampler Club was over until next Thursday from 1-3 p.m.

Later that evening, Laura Alice and Polly Esther sat on either side of the quilting frame working on the Double-Wedding-Ring quilt they had promised would be ready in June for Eunice Frank's granddaughter's wedding. Belle, lying beneath the frame, was comforted by the stockinged feet of her owners on either side of her rounded body. As usual, she dozed to the hypnotic sound of the ticking clock on the wall near-by.

Although the Sampler Club ladies had left the shop hours ago, the events of the day still troubled Polly Esther. "I didn't like all the talk about birthdays and horoscope signs at club today. I just knew it would get out of hand."

"Get out of hand! Since when is celebrating birthdays getting out of hand?" Laura Alice retorted somewhat sharply. She quickly followed with an "ouch – I stuck myself," she said as she put down her quilting needle and grabbed a handkerchief from her pocket to dab at the speck of blood before it got on the quilt.

"You know what I mean," Polly quickly replied. "The ladies are starting to read their horoscopes in the paper and it's all because of us and these heathen zodiac sampler blocks," Polly Esther emphasizing the word 'heathen.'

"You mean it's all because of me. That's what you mean," Laura Alice paused, then continued, "Sister, listen to me. We both liked the patterns. We talked about this for a month before we ordered them. The names of the blocks could have been anything. They're just star shaped designs each one a little different."

"I know, but they're named after false gods and it makes me feel guilty," Polly admitted.

"For goodness sake! I'd think you could come up with something worse than making a zodiac sampler block if you need to feel guilty," Laura continued. "Making these blocks doesn't make us heathen. You've got to get over that. You're supposed to be the one who's wise, named after Queen, Esther, you know. Forget the names of the blocks; just think of the pieces and the designs. It will be all right," Laura said, comforting her sister. Laura was the strong one, or at least the verbally bold one. Polly could never confront like Laura. She would bear her guilt in silence.

The four ladies from Sampler Club were the same ones who came regardless of what patterns the shop sisters decided to use. It wasn't that Ethel, Vesta, Nettie, or Thelma needed another quilt, or that they were learning to quilt. It was simply that quilting was what they liked to do and that they were friends. Each Thursday was Sampler Club, and had been for years.

The first Thursday of each month, the club members cut out the fabric from the patterns, the next three weeks they sat in their usual chairs hand sewing the pieces to make a block. It could have been done faster. They could have used sewing machines, but what was the hurry? It was their recreation as well as a quilting project. Sewing baskets went home, but no one tried to rush her work. Slow and steady was better than trying to outdo a quilting sister. The Capricorn and Aquarius blocks had been finished in January and February, now Pisces had begun.

"We can serve what's left of the applesauce cake tomorrow evening at game time," Polly said. "It's always flavorful and moist after a day or two. I think I'll put out a note for the milkman to leave a pint of cream. I can make topping for the cake and have some cream for the coffee."

"Wally said he was bringing Ralph Stillwell," Laura spoke. "He's probably trying to get Ralph out some since Irma's gone. Wally said he doesn't go anywhere except to the barber shop."

"I hope no one gets the wrong idea about two widowers coming here. What do you think sister?"

"Sister, really, you are such a prude anymore! I'm just too weary to worry about it. Anyway, if we all sit at the card table with the lights on and the shades up, people can see what we're doing if they care to look. Although I agree that it never hurts to be on guard of our reputations even if we are over sixty," Laura said.

"Like mother used to say, 'There's no fool like an old fool,'" Polly added. Then all was quiet while the clock measured the time.

Finally Laura spoke, "Let's not let the sun go down with us being snippy with each other. I'm sorry sister for being sassy with you earlier. Forgive me. It's time for me to rest my eyes."

"I forgive you, sister. I agree; we're both tired. Is it your turn to take Belle out?" Polly asked as her sister rose from the quilting frame, having put her needle to rest for the night.

"I took her out this morning if you remember, but I'll take care of her. You can take her out both times tomorrow. Good night sister."

Belle slowly rose from her spot under the frame to join Laura Alice on her trek outside. It seemed she understood exactly what had been said, or maybe it was just from habit. It was that time and the clock had just struck 9:00 p.m.

## CHAPTER TWO

Sisters' Sewing Shop was a beehive of activity on Friday. The two queen bees darted here and there helping customers find the right fabric for a baby quilt, new curtains, projects for a shower and wedding gifts, and who knows what. Sue Ellen Collier, Thelma's daughter came in to find fabric for a quilted table runner she wanted to make for her mother as a birthday gift. Mum was the word, of course. Ethel Connelly needed more gold colored embroidery thread, and Mable Shaffer, the postmaster's wife was trying to find fabric for new pillowcases. It needed to look right with the spread which she carried along. There was also a new order for a yellow and white gingham curtain for Clara Bates' bathroom window. Guests were coming for Easter and she wanted that room freshened before then.

Polly who did most of the cooking, nursed a pot of vegetable soup in a slow oven in the kitchen all afternoon. She had found baking the soup worked well without constant watching and before long the mouthwatering scent crept into the sewing shop giving rise to many comments from the customers.

"I don't know how you sisters get so much done," Clara Bates commented.

"You ladies could open a restaurant in here too," Hazel Croyle replied. "I nearly always get hungry if I come in the afternoon. It gives me ideas for supper though."

"I think I'd get more done if I didn't have to pick up after Virgil," Mable Shaffer added. "But I wouldn't trade him in. I shouldn't have even said that. I know how Ethel has missed Cecil."

"I know," Clara chimed in. "We can't live with them or without them."

*Sister and I have managed just fine without husbands*, Polly was thinking, but didn't say so.

Several bolts of new spring fabric were displayed in the front window along with a few new patterns and several spools of thread. It was time for spring sewing to go along with the house cleaning which had already begun. The shop was doing well and they were busy, in fact too busy. When they weren't waiting on customers, they were working on custom made projects which included the king-sized handmade quilt for the wedding in June. "If we didn't take time to rest, we could work all day and be up all night and still not get done," Polly complained.

"It's what we could call a blessed nuisance," Laura said. "We are blessed that our business is good, but sometimes it gets to be too much. At least we take off Friday evenings and Sundays. Can you imagine how surprised Mother would be if she could see the shop now."

"She surely would be. I think she would be proud of us and proud that her 'alterations' shop has come such a long way," Laura added.

Tonight Wally and Ralph would be entertained at the card table in the library. The windows in the room would be bright with the good reading light, the shades up, and all the world could see Miss Laura Alice Monroe and Miss Polly Esther Monroe playing cards, or dominoes with Wally and Ralph come 7:00 p.m.

The shade on the door was pulled and the 'closed' sign

faced out promptly at 5:00 p.m. and the last of the customers left shortly after. Laura Alice began accounting for the receipts of the day while Polly Ester straightened and replaced bolts of fabric to shelves. Finally Laura did a quick sweep of the floor while Polly Esther left for the kitchen. The sisters worked well together each knowing what needed to be done and taking the initiative to follow through.

Polly Esther served the waiting vegetable soup, after which Laura Alice washed the dishes and straightened the kitchen. With all the chores done, it was time to freshen-up and get ready for guests. Depending on the business of the day, or the time of the year, it might mean a complete change of clothes, or just a fresh blouse, hair combed, or a little lipstick, although neither usually wore much make-up.

Wally, jovial and chatty, was the usual Friday evening guest, and they always looked forward to his coming. Wally, who had been a widower for many years, looked forward to the sisters' company as well as the baked goodies they served. They played a variety of card games, yet it was up to Wally to bring another guest if they wanted four players.

Tonight he was bringing Ralph Stillwell. Neither Laura Alice, nor Polly Esther was certain how this would work. Ralph was the banker and they had never known him outside the bank. Neither he nor Irma went to church in town, nor appeared at anything locally. There had been that encounter with Irma once, but that was minor and didn't involve Ralph. He had been a widower now for most of the past year; maybe he was still in mourning, the sisters didn't know. He retired from the bank just a few months after his wife died and as usual hadn't been seen around town since, just in the barber shop. Maybe Wally could at least get Ralph to go to the other side of the street.

As they came downstairs, Laura Alice asked, "Sister, do

you have rouge on your cheeks tonight? You look a little more colorful than usual."

"Don't be ridiculous---of course not! I'm just a little heated from eating that hot soup for supper," Polly Esther replied.

"Do I smell lavender soap?" Polly Esther asked as she walked past her sister.

"I think you smell the cabbage from the vegetable soup," Laura Alice replied with a straight face.

"I can certainly tell the difference between cabbage and lavender," Polly Esther snapped, giving her sister a disapproving stare.

Just then the doorbell rang and they, and Belle hurried to greet their guests. Perhaps there was still hope for who might turn up on the doorstep since neither sister had ever married.

Ralph looking anxious stood next to Wally. He was bundled up as if he were ready to play in the snow wearing a red and black plaid cap with flaps down over his ears and a strap secure under his chin. He wore brown leather gloves and a dark green wool coat, with a fur collar. His face looked as if he were in pain, while Wally looked his usual self, bare headed, no gloves, wearing a sports jacket open in the front exposing his much rounded stomach, and as usual, a big smile.

"Evening ladies," Wally said his cheeks rosy from the cold. He stooped to greet Belle scratching behind her ears while she licked his hands. He then led the way inside while Ralph hung back. "Burr! It's cold out there," Wally continued, now rubbing his hands together. "That sun today was a fooler. I thought spring was on the way. You know my friend Ralph." Wally said looking back at Ralph who was slowly moving forward clutching a box of dominoes.

Soon Ralph was unbundled, his coat on the hall tree and gloves on the nearby table. They all moved to the library and were seated with the box of dominoes on the table. "Ralph,

I've never really played dominoes before, you'll have to get me up to speed," Wally announced. "Girls, do you know how they're played?"

"Not really. We've always had a set around the house, but we mostly played cards," Laura Alice announced. "I remember how we stood them on end next to each other then pushed the first one over to see them all fall down, but that wasn't very entertaining after a while."

"I think I played with father once where we matched the dots, but I don't remember much about it," Polly Esther added.

"They're called 'pips'," Ralph announced solemnly looking at Polly Esther.

Polly looked at the others for a clue, then back to Ralph. "What did you say?"

"I said they're called 'pips'; you called them 'dots.'"

"Oh, I see," Polly said.

"Cards are really from the devil, you know," Ralph announced. "We never played cards at our home, nor did we let Bernice play them. Irma and I were always strict about that," he added, then looked about at each as if looking for a reaction. No one said or did anything. It seemed like the beginning of a long evening.

For the next half hour Wally, Laura Alice, and Polly Esther learned all they ever wanted to know about dominoes and then some. It seems that a set of dominoes contains one unique piece for each possible combination of two ends with zero to six pips, and is known as a double-six set because the highest-value piece has six pips on each end which is a double-six.

Ralph droned on and on in a monotone voice elaborating about the pips from one to six being generally arranged as they are on six-sided dice, but because there are also blank ends having no pips there are seven possible faces, allowing 28 unique pieces in a double-six set.

Laura Alice felt that she was about to fall from her seat if she sat still and listened to this 'bean counter" banker's account of dominoes any longer. She glanced at Polly Esther who also looked in agony. Then, because she had the sudden urge to laugh, she didn't look at Wally, but instead examined her nails resting on the table before her.

"Would anyone like a piece of applesauce cake and some coffee," Polly Esther finally asked when the tension in the room was about to explode.

"I certainly would," Wally announced. "I'd like a little cream in my coffee too if you have some."

"I'll help you," Laura Alice volunteered. "Ralph, would you like some cake?"

"I'll give it a try to be sociable, but I don't eat many sweets. It's bad for your health you know. Sugary things are the worst thing for you. My Irma took such good care of me. Without her it's been hard to keep on the straight and narrow. I don't drink coffee either; that caffeine's another bad thing."

Laura Alice and Polly Esther excused themselves to the kitchen. Belle followed. "I feel so strange," Laura Alice announced to her sister. "But I don't know whether to laugh or cry."

"Me too. Why are we feeling like this? I was looking forward to this evening."

"I'm sorry I wasted my blush," Polly Esther announced. "I just feel miserable."

"I'm sorry I used my lavender soap," Laura Alice added as she hugged her sister. "Is he contagious?"

Belle whined, and Laura gave her a dog biscuit.

"Poor Irma," Polly Esther said, "and to think that she was jealous of him."

Wally ate two pieces of cake and drank two cups of coffee. "This cake is De-licious!" Wally declared. Ralph scraped the whipped cream from his cake and ate about half the dessert, then asked for a glass of water.

The party broke up about 8:30 p.m. with each expressing that it had been a busy day. The sisters never did find out about Warren, the new man at the bank, or even how Ralph was enjoying his retirement. Those things would have to wait.

Wally and Ralph had been gone nearly an hour when Laura noticed the outside entry light shining through her bedroom window. She turned on the stairway light and made her way down the stairs in her nightie. Passing by the hallway table, she picked up the pair of brown leather gloves Ralph had placed there earlier. The initials RHS were carefully hand stitched in gold thread on the cuff of each glove. Someone who could handle a needle did that, she thought. I wonder what the "H" stands for?

The gloves looked very expensive. He would surely want them back. She loved the smell of leather and raised them to her nose. There was that familiar scent, but also something else, something she hadn't smelled for a long time. Sure, she knew that. It was Old Spice after shave lotion with the spicy pine fragrance. She wasn't likely to forget the special gift the sisters had given their father at Christmas each year. The little gift pack had two items, one bottle of lotion and one of talc, something from each of them. She remembered the familiar bottles with the old time sailing ships in blue on the creamy white background and how much her father liked the gifts from his girls. She looked to the empty space in that very entryway where the Christmas tree had stood years ago in this, the same, house of her childhood. Now with her eyes closed, she inhaled the long ago scent as the vision of Christmas past played before her.

Taking the gloves with her, she turned off the outside light, then climbed the stairs to her room. The gloves went into her purse and she snapped it shut. She would likely see Wally at church on Sunday and give the gloves to him. Ralph seemed to be a fixture in Wally's shop these days. She certainly wasn't about to call Ralph about his gloves. Far be it from her to have Ralph think that she was interested in him, which in deed, she was not.

* * *

Wally parked his car beside Laura Alice and Polly Esther's at the Deerfield Community Church on Sunday morning. "Sorry things didn't go so well Friday evening," he said looking down at the gravel as they walked.

"It wasn't your fault," Polly said watching her step on the loose gravel still somewhat covered with snow. "I don't want to say anything bad. It's not anyone's fault. We're all just different people."

"Some are just more different than others," Laura added. "We'll hope to see you next Friday evening. We can play cards again. By the way, Ralph left his gloves at our house. Would you give them to him?" Laura said opening her purse and handing them to him.

"Sure will. I'll be back come Friday. Maybe I can bring someone else."

"Good morning, Floyd," Wally spoke up as he spotted a regular from the barber shop heading his way. "See you ladies later."

Vesta was playing pre-service music on the organ when Laura and Polly took their usual seats, right side of the aisle, four rows from the front. Vesta had such a wonderful touch with the music. Laura could hardly refrain from singing out whenever Vesta played a familiar tune. Thelma sat to their left in the row in front of the sisters with her daughter Sue Ellen, her husband, Homer, and Thelma's grandson, Skipper. Thelma held up her left hand for them to see that she was wearing a bandage. Sue Ellen leaned back to tell them that her mother had accidentally cut her left forefinger with her newly sharpened scissors.

The choir entered taking their places to the right front of the sanctuary and the music director came to the podium to start the service. Ethel and Nettie looked their way and smiled as they sat side by side in the alto section of the choir. All seemed right with the world. *Thanks be to God*, Polly whispered to herself.

After the music, prayer time and offering, the choir sang a vibrant version of "A Mighty Fortress is Our God" which was followed by a hearty 'Amen' from a few. Then, Pastor George moved to the podium. Although his last name, Angelopoulos, was given on the sign in front of the church, few ventured to use it. To most he was "Pastor George." His ancestors had come to this country from Greece many years ago. It was surely a long story of how he came to be in Deerfield, Indiana, but then, as Polly sometimes said, "None of us are Indians you know."

After his greeting, Pastor George stated that the text for his sermon was found in Acts 17:23. He stood silently as the sound of opening Bibles and pages being turned filled the sanctuary. After all was quiet, he then began to read:

> And Paul stood in the midst of the Areopagus and said, "Men of Athens, I observe that you are very religious in all respects. For while I was passing through and examining the objects of your worship, I also found an altar with this inscription, 'TO AN UNKNOWN GOD.' What therefore you worship in ignorance, this I proclaim to you. The God who made the world and all things in it, since He is Lord of Heaven and earth does not dwell in temples made with hands, neither is He served

by human hands as though He needed anything, since He Himself gives to all life and breath and all things.

Pastor George went on to say that some of his very ancestors were from Greece where Athens is found and were likely worshipers of the unknown and false gods Paul had spoken of. "And yet," he said, "Paul's ministry to them has not been lost. For indeed, here we sit in 1952 reading the words of Paul and knowing that they apply to us as well today. We too serve unknown gods." He went on to elaborate about how we can make gods out of most anything we make too important in our lives. He mentioned earthly treasures people seek to find satisfaction in life, only to neglect what is really important, serving the living God Paul spoke of. "God will not be found in things. God will be found in our hearts when we are centered on Him, doing His will and offering service to one another."

Polly leaned to Laura and whispered in her ear, "He's talking about the zodiac sampler, I just know it."

Laura whispered back, "Shuss, be quiet. He doesn't even know about it."

"Yes, but the Lord is giving him a message for us," Polly whispered back.

Nothing more was said about the sermon until they were in the car leaving church. Laura knew she wouldn't hear the last of it until this year and that sampler were a thing of the past.

## CHAPTER THREE

"Gracious me! That ambulance is loud and right on our street," Polly Esther said to a customer on Monday as she measured fabric to be cut. "It must have come all the way from Trenton. I wonder what's wrong."

Laura Alice, who had been standing nearby, moved to the front door, and went outside looking to the north. "Can you see anything?" Polly called anxiously looking in Laura's direction.

Laura stuck her head back through the doorway. "It looks like it's stopped in front of Ethel's place. I'm going down there to see what has happened," she called out and left.

"Will there be anything else?" Polly asked, then took the customer to the cash register to finalize the sale. The customer left and Polly followed her out the door, pulling her sweater close about her. She hurried to join her sister two houses north on the lawn at Ethel's house.

Wally Newton soon joined the sisters as they stood in silence. "What's goin' on?" he asked. "Has something' happened to that Harley fella?"

"We don't know, Wally. We just heard the ambulance," Polly responded. "It doesn't look good."

They and others who had gathered about talked in hushed tones outside the neat two story yellow frame house with the white trim. It was the one with the wrap around porch that extended across the front, the one that everyone noticed in passing through town. Ethel and Cecil Connelly had taken great pride in their home where they and their son Quinton moved from Trenton when Quinton was a youngster. They hadn't wanted Quinton to go to the big schools in Trenton and preferred to live in a small town. It had been a good move for them as they had been quickly and positively adopted by the Deerfield community.

Now both Cecil and Quinton were gone; Cecil having died several years ago from a heart attack while mowing the back lawn. Quinton died just over a year ago, coming home from Korea in a casket. Although Ethel had been proud of Quinton's service to his country, he was her only child, and now he was gone. After a while, she hired Miller's Lumberyard to remodel the back of her house to add an efficiency apartment. She said she didn't want to live alone.

Finally the ambulance attendants and Marshal Homer Collier came from the house with a sheet covered gurney followed by Harley Flynn, the renter, Ethel's nephew, who lived in the apartment in back of the house. There were loud gasps and murmurs which became louder as the procession with the gurney passed by. Harley was alternately wringing his hands and wiping his downcast eyes as he stumbled behind the marshal and ambulance attendants on the way to the ambulance.

Polly gasped aloud and hid her face in Laura's shoulder. "Oh, my Lord," she said aloud as she started to sob. "Surely this can't be real."

"We're in a bad dream," Laura said with emotion, hugging her sister with her arms about her. The tears started and would not stop as they flowed down both their faces. Each sister was now supporting the other to keep from collapsing. Wally, standing nearby, moved behind and put his wide arms about them both. "I suppose that was Ethel," he said as the threesome stood transfixed while the gurney was loaded into the ambulance.

About that time, Homer Collier raised his hands for quiet. "Folks, there's been an accident. Harley called me about an hour ago. He couldn't get Ethel to come to the door. After hollering, he went into the house, couldn't find Ethel, but saw the cellar door ajar. He found Ethel at the bottom of the steps and she didn't seem to be breathing. He called me and I called the ambulance. The body will be taken to the morgue in Trenton to try to figure out what happened here. There will be an investigation. It looks like she accidently fell down the steps onto the cement cellar floor. I reckon you might as well go home."

The crowd slowly began to disburse as the ambulance, followed by the marshal's car, with Harley seated next to the marshal left the scene. Finally, Wally spoke up. "I'm closing the shop for the rest of the day out of respect for Ethel. I need time to think about this. I think we're all in shock."

"We'll close too," Laura Alice managed to say. Polly, moving as in a trance, headed home with Laura holding her hand.

\* \* \*

The next day seemed suspended in time. The agony of their loss was upon them. It wasn't something far away, but here and now. The sisters moved about the shop dabbing at their eyes and discussing what they knew with the quilting ladies and others who stopped by. Harley, Ethel's nephew didn't seem to be at his apartment. They wondered what had happened to him.

Then Wednesday The Trenton Times contained the obituary. Now it was folded open to the obituary page on the kitchen table. Laura Alice and Polly Esther had each read the notice, but left it in place as if they had to verify from time to time that it was really true.

> DEERFIELD, Ind. Ethel Flynn Connelly, 64, of Deerfield was found dead in her home Tuesday, March 11th, from an apparent accidental fall. Town Marshal Homer Collier is investigating.
>
> Mrs. Connelly is preceded in death by her husband Cecil Connelly and her son, Quinton Connelly, who died in the Korean Conflict. She is survived by a sister, Janette Marsh, of Springfield, Ohio and a nephew, Harley Flynn. Memorial services are being arranged by Rev. George Angelopolous of the Deerfield Community Church, and Warren Haskett, her Power of Attorney from the Deerfield State Bank. The date and time of the funeral will be announced later.

"What is there to investigate?" Polly asked Laura. "Doesn't that sound like they think something isn't right? I wish we could find out what's going on."

"It will come out in good time. Right now we have to keep ourselves calm, meet with the club tomorrow and see what we can do to honor Ethel. I wish we could talk to Ethel's sister, Janette. I hope she isn't being left out of all this."

Vesta stopped by shortly after the shop opened even though the quilting club would meet the next day. "Did you see the notice in the paper? This is such a shock. I can't believe Ethel is gone. Have you heard any more about the funeral?" she asked.

"Yes, we saw it. We were down at the house when the ambulance was there," Laura said. "I can still see that covered gurney in my head. It was terrible knowing that Ethel . . ." she said before her voice trailed off. "No, Vesta, we don't know anything more, just what's in the paper," Laura said. "Maybe we'll know by club tomorrow. If you talk to Thelma or Nettie, tell them we don't know anything else."

Finally, it was closing time on what had seemed a very long day. The aroma of marzetti hot dish filled the air. Polly had started their supper nearly an hour ago when it was slow in the shop. Laura Alice was finishing up the receipts for the day while Polly Esther returned bolts to the shelves and straightened the shop in readiness for the next day. After they ate, it would be back to the quilting frame and more handwork on the Double-Wedding-Ring.

"Sister, I've been trying to think of something we can do to honor Ethel," Polly said as Laura set the table and filled the water glasses. "The thing that keeps coming to mind is that we need to finish her quilt. We could give it to her sister or to Harley in her memory. What do you think?" Polly asked. "The ladies are coming tomorrow. We could figure out how we could all work together to get it done."

"Sister, I like that idea. We could all do extra blocks to finish what she started. Then, we could put all our names on a label on the back in memory of Ethel and the date we finish it. You know sister, there's one thing I don't understand about what was in the paper."

"What's that? About the obituary you mean?"

"Yes, Ethel had told us about Harley being her nephew you know. Well, it gave her sister's name as Janette Marsh. It gave Ethel's second name as Flynn, the same as Harley's.

What do you make of that? Flynn seems to have been Ethel's maiden name."

"Let me see that paper again. I guess I didn't notice that, or didn't think anything about it," Laura said reaching for the paper again.

"I don't know what it means. I know that Ethel was my friend and I'm not going to say anything about it to anyone. It isn't a time to think badly about her or her family," Laura said after reading the obituary again.

"You know, I have another idea that just came to me," Polly said. "Let's see if Harley is home yet. Maybe he could let us into Ethel's house so we can get her sewing basket. If we had it before the ladies come tomorrow, we could tell them about finishing her quilt and have the blocks she has already completed. That would help so much. We could even see if she had enough fabric or if we'll need extra."

"We don't even know if he's there. If so, he's likely alone. I feel so sorry for him being alone at a time like this."

"Ethel never talked about Harley's problems, but she wanted to help him. She probably got that job for him at the lumber yard. We could take a hot dish of some kind to him," Laura said. "That's the least we could do."

"I agree. There's plenty of that marzetti hot dish I made for supper. We could share that," Polly said. "The funeral date and time will surely be in tomorrow's paper. We'll likely know about that before the ladies come."

Laura went on, "I'll finish in the shop. You go ahead and get Harley's food ready. Even if he's not home, it won't be any big problem. We'll just bring it back."

Polly spooned half the marzetti into a smaller casserole, put a little extra cheese on the top and put it in the oven for a while to melt. The dish was wrapped in two tea towels and placed on a tray to take to Harley.

The sisters ate their meal then bundled in coats and scarves headed two houses north past the B.P.O.E. lodge to Harley's apartment in the back of Ethel's yellow house. Polly carried the tray while Laura carried her big flashlight. Darkness still came early even though the days were lengthening.

The sky had been overcast with periods of light snow followed by what the weatherman called snizzle, a mixture of snow and drizzle. It was just that time of the year in Indiana when the season was in change. Spring would soon be born, but the labor pains were still in evidence. Laura flipped on the back porch light as the sisters left.

They took care walking on the uneven gravel of the B.P.O.E. parking lot next door. The light from the flashlight guided them safely past the large rocks painted white between the parking lot and the back entrance to the lodge. The Elks were particular about their lawn not wanting anyone to park past the gravel.

Past the parking lot, they could see a light through the window in the door of Harley's apartment in Ethel's house. They approached and Laura knocked. All was still. She knocked several more times waiting to hear steps each time. Finally Harley came to the door. He looked unkempt, his eyes swollen and auburn hair in disarray. His clothes looked as if he had worn them for days and probably slept in them too. The top button was through about the third button hole and the shirt hung at an angle.

"What you want?" Harley asked in a harsh tone while staring at the ladies.

"Harley, we were friends of your Aunt Ethel. We're so sorry about her accident. We brought you some food. May we come in?" Laura asked.

"Not clean here," Harley replied. "Maybe you go away."

"We're not worried about how your house looks, Harley. We want to help you and for you to help us too," Polly said.

Harley's hand went to his head and he smoothed his hair down. Slowly, he moved aside and the ladies went into his apartment. The back door entered into the kitchen. Dirty dishes filled the sink and counter tops. The collection must have taken longer than the past several days. The oven door was open with a pie pan of burned food, whatever it had been, on a cookie sheet. Clothes hung over the backs of chairs and lay on the floor while assorted envelopes and newspapers were scattered across the table top. *Where will I put the dish?* Polly thought.

She managed to use the edge of the tray to push papers on the table out of the way to make a place for the hot dish. The towels were unwrapped and the lid to the dish lifted. Steam rose from the dish and the aroma of the ground beef, spaghetti, and tomato casserole soon filled the room. Harley stood watching during the unveiling. "It smell good," he said. "Aunt Effel cook for me. I not good cook."

"Harley, can we help you clean up a bit?" Laura asked. "We know you have been through a shock with your Aunt's death."

"Effel want me be clean," he said as he started to cry. "I not good. I sorry."

"Harley, we would like to help you. Is Ethel's sister, Janette your mother?"

"Yes, she mother. She come tomorrow. She take me home wif her after say good-bye Aunt Effel."

"Harley, there is something you could do for us. Your Aunt Ethel was making a quilt. She liked to sew, you probably know."

"Yes, she sew for me sometime."

"We would like to get her sewing basket so that we could finish the quilt she was making."

We would give it to your mother in memory of your Aunt Ethel if we could finish it. It is surely in the house. Do you know her sewing basket?"

"I know basket. I know where is," Harley said nodding that he understood and wiped his eyes.

"Would you take us into her house so we could get it? Maybe you have a key?"

"Yes, I have key. We could go down cellar to her house if you want," Harley said.

"Is that how you usually go?" Laura asked.

"Most times," he said slowly. "Sometimes I go to door and knock," he added.

"What way do you want to go now?"

"I want go door now. Cellar bad place where Aunt Effel hurt," Harley answered.

"Let's go that way then. Do you have a key?"

"Key under rock by step."

The threesome made their way around to the front of the house where Harley got the key and unlocked the door. He flipped on the switch inside by the door and the lamp on the table in front of the window came on. The ladies entered.

Everything seemed as orderly as they knew Ethel had left it. It didn't take long to spot Ethel's large sewing basket on the floor near her chair by the fireplace. Polly walked to the basket and opened it to see the familiar shades of blue and apple green fabric. Ethel used those colors in some way in nearly every quilt she made. Sometimes they would be found in prints, but this time mostly solids. It didn't take long for Laura's quick eyes to spot familiar brown gloves on the nearby side table. While Polly was looking at the fabric, Laura lifted the gloves. Sure enough, they were embroidered in gold fancy stitching with RHS on each of the cuffs. She lifted them to her nose and again smelled the scent of Old Spice. She knew the owner. *Should I leave them or take them? What should I do?*

"See these gloves, Polly," she said to her sister as she held them up.

Why had Ralph Stillwell been here? And when? Wally must have given the gloves back to Ralph. Ethel died on Monday. Does Ralph know something about what happened to Ethel?

Both Harley and Polly were now looking at her as she held the gloves. "I'll just put these back where I found them," she said laying the gloves back on the table, in the last minute decision.

With the sewing basket now in hand Polly thanked Harley. Then, the sisters made their way silently across the back lawn and parking lot to their own back door. It was even darker now and probably more overcast as neither the moon nor stars were visible. The wind was brisk as it had been when they walked the other way; now, perhaps even more cutting as they faced into it. Polly carried the sewing basket on her left arm with her head down and her right hand in her coat pocket. Laura carried the tray and managed to pull the corner of her scarf over her nose and mouth as the March wind swirled about her. By the time they got past the B.P.O.E. lodge parking lot, they were both shivering.

Belle greeted them at the door with her usual barks and cheery dance. "Poor baby, we've been neglecting you the last few days," Polly said as she stooped to rub her neck and back. "I'll get a biscuit for you."

"Sister, how can you think of a biscuit for Belle at a time like this?"

"What do you mean 'a time like this.' What time are you talking about?"

"I mean those gloves. You know who they belong to don't you?" Laura asked.

"How should I know? Maybe they belonged to Ethel," Polly said getting the biscuit for Belle.

"Didn't you see the monogrammed initials RHS on them? I smelled them. They had the same Old Spice scent as Ralph's. They were the same ones he left here on Friday night! I gave them to Wally on Sunday. Ralph or Wally had to be at Ethel's sometime after that."

"I'm sorry, I wasn't thinking. I was so excited to get the basket, I wasn't paying too much attention to what you were doing with the gloves," Polly replied. "What do you think about the gloves?"

"I don't know. I didn't know whether I should have taken them or not. You know Marshal Collier is investigating. Maybe he should know about the gloves."

"You don't think Ralph had anything to do with Ethel falling down the steps do you? Why would he want to hurt Ethel? I don't know if he even knew her very well."

"He probably knew her from the bank, but why was he there?"

"Sister, that sounds plain nosey of you. Maybe he was paying a social call. It wouldn't be a crime you know," Polly added.

"I just want to know what happened to Ethel, and Ralph may know more than you would like to believe."

"I find it hard to believe that the Ralph Stillwell who was at our house on Friday is a shady character. Sister, he's a 'mouse' if you ask me. I'm glad you didn't take those gloves. Just leave well enough alone," Polly said as she marched off to the library with the sewing box in hand. "I'm going to see what Ethel has in here and how much fabric is left toward finishing the blocks. Then I'm going to bed, tomorrow will be a busy day."

Laura couldn't turn things off like her sister. Something isn't right. Ralph at Ethel's right before she died, or maybe he was there when she died. Harley's last name is Flynn, the same as Ethel's maiden name. Harley saying his mother is Janette, yet her last name isn't Flynn. Could Harley really be Ethel's son? Was Harley born before she married? Maybe I am nosey, but something isn't right.

The flood of repeats of what she had heard during the last three days and questions she couldn't answer continued to splash about in her mind. Ethel wasn't frail. She was hearty. How could she just fall down the steps?

In the kitchen Laura attacked the pile of dirty dishes. Polly had cooked, she, at least, could clean. In their haste to take the dish to Harley, no water had been added to the sticky goo left from the cheese sauce. She now attacked the hardened remains with hot water, a Brillo pad, dish soap and muscle. One thing she knew, nosey or not, she would get some answers. Whether it was a pan that needed cleaning, or a friend's death, she wouldn't give up.

The questions continued through the night as she struggled to sleep. She wasn't sure whether she was awake or asleep when she pictured Ralph, eating carrots and radishes with Ethel. Then Harley and Ralph were with Ethel in the kitchen as she poured tall glasses of milk, Ralph picking up his glass while wearing his leather embroidered gloves.

She saw the ladies from the Sampler Club gathered in the shop, the clock ticking as each lady admired her new Bavarian Whetstone. Ethel spoke up, "My horoscope said that I must be cautious. Will the whetstone hurt me?"

"No. It's just a smooth stone. It isn't a weapon," Vesta said.

"That Warren is so handsome. He reminds me of my Cecil," Ethel said. "Did you ladies see any resemblance? I miss Cecil so. I think I'll go to the bank after club meeting."

"Do you want applesauce cake, Ethel?"

"Will it hurt me?" Ethel asked.

"No, Ethel, it won't hurt you," Polly said.

"But my horoscope said to the cautious," Ethel said. "I don't know what might hurt me."

## CHAPTER FOUR

Polly was up and dressed before Laura awoke Thursday. It was an hour before the shop would open. Laura, still in her nightie, was pouring corn flakes into a bowl when Polly came into the kitchen with the newspaper. "The funeral is Saturday at 10:00 at the church with viewing an hour before," Polly announced. "We'll close the shop of course. We need to get flowers. Maybe the ladies would want to go in with us. They could be from the Sampler Club."

"That sounds fine to me. We'll have to call long distance to Pretty Posey in Trenton to order. I don't think they deliver out of town," Laura added. "They'd have to be picked up Friday before they close. We'd better check how late they're open."

"They may not have much this time of the year. We could get a Peace Lily. Janette could take that home after the service."

"We'll ask the ladies."

"You didn't sleep well last night did you?" Polly asked. "Are you still thinking about those gloves?"

"My head was spinning. I kept hearing Harley, how he talked at Ethel's house. We'd never really talked to him before. We just knew who he was. Then last night I kept thinking, we don't really know much about him. We just know he's Ethel's nephew. At least I think that's who he is. We don't know about his problem. Maybe we don't have to know, but I'd like to anyway. I don't suppose he's dangerous. Then Ralph telling about dominoes, and Marshal Collier talking about an investigation, the gloves, and the obituary. Poor Ethel, I'm just so upset, I don't know what to think. I keep asking myself if someone did something to cause her to fall down the stairs. Did she just fall for some other reason? Did she have a stroke or a dizzy spell? We didn't think of Ethel as frail, but we're all getting older you know. Was she pushed? Who would want to hurt her? Did Harley push her? I don't have any answers, just questions. To answer your question, I hardly slept at all."

"Take your time getting to the shop. I know how you feel. I'm upset too, but at least I slept. I can handle things this morning. The club will be here at one. That won't be easy. They're upset like we are. We can talk about the memory quilt for Ethel's family, maybe that will help."

"Thank you sister, I need a little quiet time. I'm thankful you haven't blamed me for Ethel's death," Laura said rather quietly.

"Why would I blame you? What did you do?" Polly asked looking point blank at Laura.

"You know. . . the zodiac patterns. I talked you into it. Now it's Ethel's sign and she died, even on her birthday, if you noticed. I was so sure it was all just superstitious nonsense to even think about the zodiac having anything to do with our lives. Do you remember Ethel saying that her horoscope told her to be cautious? I can't get that out of my mind. Maybe all this is because of me?" Laura couldn't bring herself to look at Polly as she spoke. Her head was down looking into the bowl of cornflakes which she nervously continued to stir.

"Sister, you know how I felt, but I don't blame you. It hadn't even entered my mind. I don't know what I thought would happen. . . just something bad. Maybe this would have happened anyway. We don't even know if it was an accident or not," Polly said patting her sister on the shoulder then bending to give her a hug.

"We can try to find out what really happened. Maybe it wasn't our fault at all. . . I'll help you." Polly said as she turned to leave for the shop. Laura returned to her flakes which by now were mush. Somehow it helped to know that Polly didn't blame her and that they would work together to find out what happened to Ethel. She needed answers.

All the Sampler Club ladies came early. Laura had held a cold washcloth to her eyes before going to face the ladies. It didn't seem to matter a great deal because everyone else looked blurry eyed and sad too. Everyone hugged each of the others and wiped away more tears. It was quiet until Polly spoke.

"Ladies, we've had a shock. One of our own has been taken away. I know Ethel wouldn't want us to grieve for long. Maybe we could take a while to remember some things about our dear friend that would help. Would anyone like to share?" she asked.

Tearfully, Nettie, hanky in hand, began, "You know that Ethel and me sang in the choir at church. I never thought I could sing a lick until Ethel encouraged me to join the choir. She said she would help me, and she did. They say I sing alto, but I never could have without Ethel. I don't know what I'll do now."

Vesta seated next to her took her hand. "Nettie, you know she would want you to sing. You'll do fine." Vesta went on, "I never felt I could choose fabrics very well. Ethel showed me that color wheel and helped me get my color sense together."

"Ethel was good with colors, that's for sure," Thelma continued. "She helped me too. You know how she used color in her house, such pretty curtains, and pillows. It looked like a magazine. I'll miss her so much," she said, wiping her eyes and nose. "You could tell Ethel a secret, anything at all, and you knew she would never tell."

"Ethel was our friend and neighbor with just the Elks between us. We all saw that Ethel was talented and kind. She didn't make a big deal out of helping others, but she surely did. You know how she helped Harley. She cooked for him and helped him get that job, but she never went on about it. She helped everybody.

"Polly and me have been thinking about what we could do to show how much we cared for Ethel. Maybe we can do one last thing." Laura said. "It was Polly's idea, so I'll let her tell you."

Polly picked up Ethel's sewing basket from beside her. "That's her basket!" Nettie called out. "Where did you get it?"

"Laura Alice and me took a hot dish to Harley last evening and asked him to let us in Ethel's house so we could get it. He let us in, and we took it. I don't think it was stealing. We had an idea."

After hearing the plan, all the ladies agreed to finish Ethel's quilt and give it to her sister at a later date.

Polly opened the lid of the basket and took out the completed blocks and extra folded fabric from the top. "It looks like we'll need more fabric," she said. She began to take out the other sewing items one by one. "We could pass her sewing basket around when it's each person's turn to piece a block," she continued. "That would make it extra special, like Ethel was right there with you." Everything was out on the table now including her scissors, thread, thimble, extra needles, measuring tape, and pin cushion with pins. "I wonder what happened to her Bavarian Whetstone? She put it there just last week. It should be here, but it's not," Polly finally said.

"You'd think it would be there," Vesta said. "She got hers the same time we got ours."

"Well, there's no need to worry about that. We can use ours if we need to sharpen," Nettie added. "It's just strange that it isn't here."

Laura Alice and Polly Esther agreed to donate any extra fabric needed. Assignments were made on who would make which extra blocks. While the quilt wouldn't be finished right away, they would let Ethel's sister know it was on the way and would be sent to her when finished.

Nothing was said about the 'curse of the zodiac' and the sisters weren't about to bring it up. Flowers were ordered and Nettie volunteered to pick them up in her Hudson on Friday afternoon and take them to the church in time for the viewing on Saturday.

Extra fabric for the next block was measured and given out. When all was settled, each took out her own handwork and set about piecing for the remainder of the meeting. It was comforting to be together even if it wasn't like usual. The next challenge would be the viewing, the funeral and saying goodbye to Ethel.

Nettie lingered after the others had left from club. "I wanted to tell you something Ethel told me. It's probably not important, but it's been on my mind and I want to tell someone," Nettie continued.

"We know you were close to Ethel," Laura said taking Nettie's hand.

"It's about her boy, Quinton," Nettie said. "Ethel told me a secret about him. I guess I can tell you now. She said he was adopted. Did you know that?"

"Well, no, I didn't," Laura said, "Did you know that, Polly?" She said now looking to her sister who nodded her head no.

"She said she hadn't told many people, but she told me. I was telling her how much I wished Bert and me had children but that I couldn't conceive. She said she understood and had been in the same situation. Then she went on to tell me that a relative of hers who was unmarried found out that she was pregnant."

"I would never have guessed," Polly said. "She seemed so devoted to Quinton. "I'm sure she loved him just as much as if he was born to her."

"There's one thing I'm still puzzling about," Nettie said.

"What's that?" Laura asked.

"She said something about Quinton having a brother she wished she had taken too."

"Quinton had a brother?" Polly asked.

"I think that's what she said. I should have asked more, but it seemed so private and I didn't want to question beyond what she wanted to tell me. You know how private Ethel was. You could trust her with anything, and she was trusting me by telling about adopting Quinton.

"It's at a time like this that all those little things about a person come back," Nettie went on. "We never talked about it again, but she knew how much I wished I had had a child. I think she wanted me to know that adopting a child was a good thing, but it was too late for me and Bert to do that either," Nettie said.

"Thank you for trusting us with this," Polly said. "You know, we don't have children either, not even husbands. We understand."

\* \* \*

A light snow had fallen Friday night, yet it was sunny Saturday morning when Laura Alice and Polly Esther pulled their Ford into the church parking lot. They recognized Nettie's Hudson and parked next to it. Wally's Chevy was on the other side of Nettie's car.

Ezra Fritz from Waldron Brother's Funeral Home greeted

them at the door. There was finality when Ezra greeted you at the door whether at the church or the funeral home. Ezra, thin and gaunt, was in his usual black suit with black string tie. His face, as always, was somber matching the occasion while he directed the viewers to the registry and into the sanctuary. "I think Ezra will greet us at the Pearly Gates someday," Laura whispered to Polly after they had moved on.

Wally came forward to greet them. "That lady sitting on the front row to the right is Janette, Ethel's sister. She came from Ohio. She's by herself. Harley is her boy. I'm not gonna stay. I don't take these kinds of things very well. I just wanted to pay my respects," he said before he moved toward the door they had just entered.

"I've never seen Wally so befuddled," Laura said. "He actually looked pale."

"I don't think any of us wants to be here, but we'll stay anyway. Poor Wally, he's taken this harder than we know," Polly replied.

As the sisters moved toward the casket, they became aware of Harley seated next to a white haired man at the far left end of the first row, on the other side of the sanctuary from Janette. They soon recognized the man. It was Ralph Stillwell. Harley with his head bent toward Ralph was wiping his eyes with his hands. Ralph took a handkerchief from his coat pocket and handed it to Harley. Harley accepted it and put it to use. The sister's looked on in amazement. How did Ralph happen to know Harley so well? Here they sat like old friends.

"Hello," the tall stylishly dressed lady said as she approached. "I'm Janette Marsh, Ethel's sister. Thank you for coming."

"I'm Laura Alice Monroe, a friend of Ethel's and this is my sister, Polly Esther."

"We have the sewing shop where Ethel came each week,"

Polly continued. "We are so sorry about Ethel's accident. We can hardly believe she's gone."

"It was a shock to all of us. Harley is beside himself," Janette said. "Ethel has often spoken of you both to me."

"We took a hot dish to Harley," Laura added. "He said you would be taking him home with you."

"He told you that!" Janette said abruptly.

"Yes, we know he enjoyed living in the apartment with Ethel, but things are different now with Ethel gone," Polly said.

"Ethel didn't tell you about Harley did she?" Janette asked.

"No, she didn't speak much about him, and we didn't ask," Laura Alice said.

"Well, I don't know you ladies, but it's no secret. Harley was in a home for disabled before Ethel brought him here. He didn't live with me. He has never really lived with me. This complicates things," Janette said.

"You're his mother aren't you?" Polly asked.

"I gave birth to Harley if that's what you mean," Janette said looking in his direction as he sat next to Ralph. "My husband isn't Harley's father. He has never accepted Harley with his disabilities."

"I'm so sorry," Laura Alice said. "We didn't know."

"We're not meaning to pry into your business," Polly added.

"Ethel and I were very different even if we were sisters. When she lost Quinton in Korea, she wanted Harley to come to live with her. It was all right by me. In fact, I welcomed it. Ethel would be good to him, and Blaine would stop complaining to me about the cost for keeping him in the home where he lived."

"We would like to move to the casket to say good bye to Ethel if you don't mind," Laura said. It was becoming too personal for her to grasp. What will become of Harley? They were both thinking.

"Sure, go ahead. I'll stay here to greet others. I'd like to talk with you both later," she said as they started to move ahead.

Others made their way into the church past the casket, and took seats in the sanctuary. Vesta took her seat at the organ and began to play, signaling the start of the funeral. Pastor George walked to the pulpit, gave the text for his message, opened his Bible and looked at those gathered before him. He announced, "We have gathered here today to honor the life of our dear sister, Ethel Flynn Connelly."

Everyone now looked to the far end of the front row as Harley let out a loud sound, "Waah, Waah!" crying from the depths of his heart. Ralph seated next to him placed his arm about Harley's shoulder patting him. Harley was quieted.

Pastor George looking at his text again continued. "Ethel was born on March 10th, 1887 in Celina, Ohio to Frazier and Della Flynn. She is preceded in death by her husband, Cecil, and their son, Quinton. She is survived by her sister, Janette Marsh, and nephew, Harley Flynn."

Attention was diverted a second time as Harley again voiced a loud, "Waah, Waah!" while rubbing his eyes and wiping his nose. Ralph again leaned toward him, his arm about his shoulder and drew him closer whispering something in his ear. Harley became quiet and Pastor George resumed.

The ceremony moved slowly with Harley's continued outbursts. Janette, who had been fidgeting, could take no more. All were hushed, looking at Harley after another outburst when Janette, seated by herself at the other end of the front row stood. Now everyone looked in her direction, "Harley, I have had just about enough of you!" she yelled staring in his direction. "Either be quiet, or get yourself out of here! Do you hear me?" She continued to stand, the challenger not to be dismissed.

Rising, Harley and Ralph proceeded to walk to the exit near their side of the room never once looking in the challenger's direction. Janette was seated in victory, and Pastor George looked as if he wished he were anywhere else. Neither sister could remember what he said after that, except when he announced that the ladies of the church had prepared a funeral dinner to honor Ethel. All friends and family were invited to the fellowship hall to partake.

"Sister, should we stay," Polly asked. "I have never been to such a funeral."

"I think we should, sister," Laura replied. "Think of Ethel. We will do this for her."

The quiet group filed past the food counter in the fellowship hall with each taking a plate served with a slice of ham loaf, scalloped potatoes, and green beans. Individual salads, baskets of rolls, and squares of chocolate cake were already placed with the table service on small round tables spread with white cloths. The church ladies, including Nettie and Thelma, had worked to provide the meal as a part of their good-bye.

"I feel like I'll choke on food, I'm so upset," Polly whispered to Laura as they placed their plates on a table.

"Don't look now, but Janette is headed our way with her plate in hand," Laura said. "We must be cordial, sister."

"I'll bet you ladies think I'm a witch, don't you?" Janette said as she situated herself beside Polly. Not waiting for a reply to her question, she continued. "This is one of the worst days of my life. I can tell you that!"

"You can see why I can't take Harley home with me, can't you?" Janette went on. "It would just never work. Blaine has his insurance business in the front of our house. Harley would interfere with everything. It would be a disaster."

Polly and Laura looked at their plates and listened. Laura

buttered her roll and nibbled.

"I can't get him into that home where he used to stay right away. He has to be on a waiting list. Can you imagine that? It could take months. I'm frantic. You can see that can't you?"

"We can see you're very upset," Laura said. "All this has been very difficult, I'm sure."

"You don't know the half of it. Harley's almost thirty years old, don't you know. His birthday is April 1st. He can surely do for himself by now. Ethel did a lot for him, but he really needs just a little help to manage on his own. He has a job you know."

"We had no idea how old he was," Polly said, poking about at her salad.

"I might as well just ask, no need to mince around, would you ladies watch after Harley if I leave him in his apartment? It's just a few doors down from you past that B.P.O. E. place. He wouldn't be any bother. He could still go to work and live on his own. He would just have you ladies to help in case he needed someone."

Polly and Laura looked at each other with questioning eyes. "We have our business you know, the sewing shop. It keeps us quite busy," Laura finally said.

"Well, it probably wouldn't be forever. Ethel planned to leave the house to him. He could sell it and live somewhere else. Ethel told me just last week that she had a Power of Attorney at the bank. She was so excited about it. That man from the bank could work with Harley too. Would that make a difference?"

"I don't know," Polly responded. "Perhaps we could look after him until you could make other arrangements, until the home where he lived before had room for him. How does that sound to you, sister?"

"I don't think we could commit to long term, Janette,"

Laura said. "But Ethel thought a great deal of Harley and he was able to help her some. I suppose we could do that for a few months."

"That would be such a relief to me. I don't know where else to turn. He's so much like his father, but then, what's done is done. I'll go tell him; then, I'm going to head for home as soon as I can. It's a long drive you know." Janette ate some of her cake and gulped down a swallow of coffee leaving the rest of her food untouched.

Harley was seated at one of the round tables with Pastor George and Ralph Stillwell. He was obviously enjoying his food. Polly and Laura looked in his direction as Janette hurried across the room. Both sisters were wondering what Harley had eaten since Ethel's accident. The hot dish they had taken was no doubt gone. They were also both wondering what they had let themselves in for.

The funeral was over, Ethel was gone, Janette was gone, and Harley remained. Before Laura Alice and Polly Esther left the funeral, Warren Haskett, from the bank, asked the sisters to meet him along with Harley at the bank on Monday morning at 9:00 a.m. He said that he needed to finalize his responsibilities to Ethel which included provisions for Harley.

The sisters agreed. They could meet at 9:00 a.m. and hope to open the shop by 10:00. A sign on the door should handle being an hour late in case anyone showed up earlier. Ralph volunteered to take Harley home with him for the night. It seems Harley had already stayed with him the night after the accident. The sisters invited them both to eat dinner with them on Sunday after the sisters got home from church.

Thelma and Nettie insisted the sisters take leftover ham loaf, scalloped potatoes, and green beans, as well as salad and chocolate cake home with them. "That should handle Sunday dinner with your guests," Nettie said.

Vesta joined in to insist that the sisters also take home the Peace Lily purchased for Ethel's funeral. All the ladies of the club could see it each week and remember peaceful Ethel. Vesta even mentioned that Harley should get the memory quilt they were planning to make instead of Janette. "It would mean more to him," she said.

## CHAPTER FIVE

"I felt as plain as a fence post next to her," Polly finally said breaking the silence as the sisters drove home from the funeral. Miss Laura was driving and Miss Polly was seated next to her.

"I know what you mean," Laura replied. "But, I think that saying goes, 'she's as ugly as a fence post.'"

"Oh dear me, I don't think we're actually ugly are we sister?"

"No, I don't think so, but we are plain compared to her. She's what Wally would call a 'looker', I suppose."

"Where do you think she got that dress?" Polly asked. "What color would you call it?"

"Well for one thing, she didn't get it in Deerfield, and for another, she didn't make it herself," Laura replied. "I would call it some kind of purple, maybe pomegranate. That peplum that went from the neckline to below the waist made it look like a party dress to me. I've never even seen anything like that even in the magazines."

"I reckon not. You know, I don't understand men. They look at the package instead of what's inside," Polly said. "What a waste!"

"Would you like to look like that?"

"No," Polly answered, "And I'm not just being jealous either."

"Me neither," Miss Laura sighed as she pulled the car into

the drive in back of their home and shop.

"Now to get all these left overs and that Peace Lilly into the house. I hope we have room in the Frigidaire," Laura said. "It will surely come in handy tomorrow with our guests. I'm not in the mood to cook."

Saturday evening after a light supper the sisters would be found bent over the quilting fame working on the Double-Wedding-Ring quilt. It was a relief from the stress of the day as well as a time to quietly reflect.

"Sister, do you remember Elmer Priddy?" Polly Esther asked.

"You mean that boy from your class?" Laura Alice responded.

"Yes, you surely don't forget him," Polly returned.

"Well, no, I remember," Laura replied. "He was just here during high school, wasn't he?"

"Yes, I can still see him, such big brown eyes, and dark hair. I remember how Miss Simms, the English teacher called the role every day . . . last name first, then the first. She would say 'Monroe,' then 'Polly Esther,' for me. 'Priddy' was next on her list. She would say, 'Priddy,' then 'Elmer.' You know what it sounded like. There were often snickers. Some of the boys would call him 'Pretty Elmer' outside of class."

"There was a fight about that once wasn't there?"

"Yes, Elmer had taken all he wanted to hear of it. It didn't help either that he had such nice dimples when he smiled."

"You had a crush on him, didn't you?" Laura Alice asked.

"Well, yes, I did. I told Elmer once that I liked his name. He thanked me. Secretly I used to write my name as Mrs. Polly Esther Priddy on scraps of paper, just for fun."

"I found one of those didn't I?"

"Yes, and you showed it to Mother."

"I'm sorry sister," Laura said. "I remember how Mother

scolded you."

"I remember how you kept calling me 'Pretty Polly' when Mother wasn't around, and then made squawking noises like a parrot."

"You have to admit, it was kind of funny," Laura said with a chuckle. "But I'm sorry I hurt your feelings."

"Mother said Elmer's father didn't amount to much, and Elmer would be just like him. I don't remember what his father did. I think he collected scrap metal or some such thing. She said they weren't likely to stay around here and that they were 'hunkies,' not educated people like we were," Polly said. "Elmer was smart in school. He wasn't a 'hunkie.' I wonder what ever happened to him? I wonder if he still has those dimples?" Polly said looking in the distance with a look of regret as she remembered.

"We had our chances, sister, but they're gone now. Nobody was good enough," Laura Alice added. "Do you remember Lester Frazer?"

"He was a little older than you wasn't he?" Polly asked.

"Yes, just a year. Remember his red hair and freckles?" Laura Alice recalled. "He was tall and strong too. He could outrun anybody. Mother said we would never want to get red hair started in the family, it would last for generations. Somehow that was a bad thing to her. I liked red hair. Still do."

"We never spoke up when we were young, we would never have been sassy. We just listened and did what we were supposed to do. Father never spoke up either about what Mother said. She was in charge of us girls," Polly said.

"Father was always reading or writing in the library, you know. We were to be quiet and not disturb his preparation for teaching. He relived the past so he could tell it to his students." Laura recalled.

"We had good parents," Polly said maybe feeling a bit guilty speaking so about her parents. The clock struck nine. She put her thimble down and parked her needle for the night.

"Yes, our parents were good, but I wish some things had been different," Laura said as she too put her stitches aside until another day.

"People come and go in our lives. Only the memories remain. Ethel has gone now, but her memory remains. I have mostly good memories about all those who have gone. Goodnight, sister. I'll take Belle out," Polly said.

* * *

Sunday morning at church was like going through the motions, neither sister felt like going anywhere. "We have to go, others are counting on us being there, just like we are counting on them," Polly reminded Laura. "It takes time to heal."

Vesta played the organ without the usual expression she was known to add. Nettie sang in the choir without her helpmate, wiping her eyes occasionally throughout the anthem, and Thelma sat as usual with her daughter and son-in-law, Homer Collier, the marshal. Later Thelma said that Skipper was home with a sore throat, and his dad had run the paper route for him. Each seemed in their own solitary world of sadness doing what needed to be done. There were hushed greetings and few smiles exchanged. It was a church in mourning.

Pastor George spoke of Christian friendship and showing appreciation for those we love. He used as his text I Corinthians, chapter 13. He read the words of long ago that spoke of love being patient, kind, not jealous, not bragging, nor arrogant. "Love bears all things, believes all things, hopes all things, and endures all things," he said. "Even in times of distress, we can still show love. Love never fails," he finally concluded.

Laura Alice and Polly Esther thanked Pastor George for

the message as they left and quietly made their way to the car. "I know he was talking about Ethel," Laura Alice said. "She was such an example of what he was talking about."

"He was encouraging all of us to be like her," Polly Esther added. "We must remember that with our guests at dinner today. I'm not looking forward to having Ralph Stillwell in our house as a guest again so soon, although he did seem kind and thoughtful to Harley."

Ralph and Harley were waiting in Ralph's dark green Studebaker in front of the house when they came past before pulling around the corner to drive into their drive in back. "Leave it to Ralph to be early and make us rush getting things ready. I'm already feeling frustrated with him and he's not even in the house yet," Laura Alice spouted what she was thinking.

"Be patient and kind, sister," Polly Esther said. "Remember the message this morning."

"I'm trying, sister. I'm trying. I just don't feel like being sociable with Ralph Stillwell."

Miss Laura went in the back door and soon came out the front to Ralph's car and knocked on the side window. Harley rolled the pane down. "You might as well get out and come on in," she said.

"You'll have to wait until we get dinner warmed. We're having leftovers from the funeral dinner." With that said, she returned to the house.

When the men were inside, Laura directed them to the library where they could look at books until the meal was ready. Belle went in to join the men. The sisters hustled about in the kitchen reheating the food. Finally, they were all seated at the kitchen table. Ralph started to pick up his napkin when Laura Alice spoke sharply, "We say grace at our house before we eat." At that Ralph put his napkin down and waited for instructions.

"Aunt Effel and me say grace," Harley said.

"Would you like to say the grace that you and Ethel used to pray?" Polly asked.

Harley took Ralph's hand and Polly's on his left side. "Everybody close eyes," he said, "and not peek." He bowed his head and began.

> "Thank you for the world so sweet. Thank you for
> the food we eat. Thank you for the birds that sing,
> Thank you Lord for everything. Amen."

"That was a nice prayer, Harley," Polly said. "Let's eat."

There was the flutter of dishes being passed and everyone started to eat. Finally, Laura spoke up, "Ralph, did Wally give you the gloves you left at our house when you came over to play games?"

"What gloves?" he said looking up at her.

"They were brown leather gloves with the initials RHS embroidered on them," Laura continued. "I assumed they were yours, although I don't know what the H stands for."

"Oh, those. No, I wondered what happened to them. You gave them to Wally?"

"Yes, I thought he would give them to you."

"He must have forgotten. I'll ask him about them."

Conversation was somewhat strained and seemed to focus mostly on the sunshine and warmer weather. Finally Polly spoke up, "We've got some of that chocolate cake for dessert. Since you don't like sweets, Ralph, maybe you would like an apple."

"Who said I don't like sweets? I'll take the cake," Ralph replied. "The H stands for Harlan."

"What did you say?" Polly asked.

"I'll take the cake," Ralph repeated. "I'm learning to like sweets once in a while."

"No, what did you say after that?"

"I said the H stands for Harlan. That was my father's name. I was named after him," Ralph said as Polly handed him a piece of chocolate cake. *What is the connection between Harley and Ralph Harlan Stillwell?* Both sisters were thinking.

Dinner was finally over. Both Ralph and Harley thanked the ladies for the invitation and the meal even if it was left overs. "It's better than I usually get," Ralph added. "My Irma was a good cook, but that's all over now."

"Harley, that man from the bank, Warren, wants to see us in the morning at 9:00 a.m.," Laura said. "He said he is finalizing your Aunt Ethel's wishes. He wants to see my sister and me and you. We don't really know what this is about, but we plan to go. We think you should go too. Should we give you a call about eight o'clock to get you awake? I assume you'll be back in your apartment tonight."

"Warren Haskett is my son-in-law you know," Ralph added. "He's married to my daughter Bernice. He's a smart fella. Good for the bank. You all need to go."

"I go home to my bed. Aunt Effel get me up for work. Will I go work?" Harley asked.

"I'll take care of your work, Harley," Ralph spoke up. "You can go to work after you get finished at the bank. Can you do that? Remember Aunt Ethel won't be there to wake you up."

"I ride bicycle to work. I know way," Harley replied.

"You will go to the bank first though Harley," Ralph added. Harley was shaking his head in agreement.

Ralph and Harley left with the understanding that the ladies would call Harley on the phone in the morning and see him at the bank at nine o'clock.

The dishes were done, both sisters took brief naps, went to Sunday evening service at the church and were ready for bed by nine o'clock. "Tomorrow will be a big day, sister. Would you mind taking Belle out tonight? I know it's my turn, but I'm so very tired," Polly added.

"I don't mind at all. You mostly took care of the dinner.

You know, Belle seemed to take up with Harley today. Did you notice that?" Laura asked and Polly nodded in agreement.

"I think he slipped her some ham loaf a couple of times," Polly added. That said, Polly left the final care of Belle to Laura and went up the back stairs to her room.

The back stairs connected the kitchen to the second floor hallway. The sisters used those stairs more than the more formal sweeping front stairs which came down in the sewing shop. The front stairs were beautiful with their sweeping bannister, but took space they would have preferred to use for the shop. Most generally a quilt or two was draped over the bannister, but those stairs were mostly ornamental.

Polly was in sweet repose when Laura tiptoed into her room some hours later, quietly calling her name and bending beside her bed to shake her shoulder. "Sister, wake up," she said in a hushed tone. "I think someone is in the house. Sister, wake up," she repeated with urgency until Polly opened her eyes and stared at her. Faint moonlight filtered through the lacy curtains giving a ghostly dimension to Laura as Polly tried to regain her bearings. "I think I heard noises downstairs, and I heard Belle. She didn't bark, just kind of whined."

Rousing herself, Polly asked, "Did you lock the back door when you brought her in from outside?"

"I don't know. I think I did, but I'm not sure. I don't remember," Laura responded. "I've got my flashlight. I think we should look. Go down with me. It might be that the wind just blew in the door if it didn't close very well. Will you go?" Laura asked.

Lifting herself now on one elbow, Polly turned back the covers and swung her legs over the side of the bed. "What choice do I have? I reckon I'm awake now. We should have a weapon just in case it's a burglar."

"Don't say that," Laura continued. "What do you think we

should take?"

"Let's go down the back stairs. There's a skillet in the oven. We could get that. You can give me the flashlight, and you get the skillet," Polly replied.

"Sister, I don't think I should take the skillet. After all, it's my flashlight," Laura quietly returned.

"Oh, all right if I must. But if I have to hit someone, you can hit them too with that big flashlight," Laura whispered.

Their plan in place, the sisters quietly descended the back steps from the north end of the upstairs hallway, most of the old wooden steps creaking as they made their way down. Finally, they opened the door to the kitchen. The outside door was closed, but unlocked. Laura shined the light about the room and settled it on the kitchen range while Polly squeaked open the oven door and took out the iron skillet.

Together they moved through the kitchen with the flashlight and skillet. Nothing was out of place so far except that Belle was not on her bed near the kitchen table.

The door to the library on the left was open and from the doorway Laura shined the light about the room. Nothing seemed amiss until she did a double take with the light on the sofa on the far left side of the room. It was the space with no bookcases, with the picture of father and mother smiling immediately above the sofa. Now the sofa was covered with a quilt, one of the quilts from the stairway bannister. It wasn't the quilt alone that caught their attention. There seemed to be a form beneath the quilt and Belle was asleep on the floor in front of the sofa.

Polly drew back outside the doorway. "Oh sister, there's something, or someone under that quilt. What shall we do? Should we call the marshal?"

"Oh no, sister," Laura replied. "He'd come down here with his siren on and wake up the neighborhood. We wouldn't want that.

"I think we should go over there. If it's a person, at least they aren't doing us any harm," Laura continued. "I'll go first, you come right behind me with the skillet. Get ready to swing it when I shine the light up close," she whispered. With that said, she started slowly through the doorway.

"Oh sister, is this wise?" Polly asked, but perhaps Laura didn't even hear. She was still on the move creeping closer to the sofa with the flashlight focused on the same.

Now they were standing beside the sofa with the lump under the quilt. Belle had roused and was looking up at the sisters but making no noise. The light revealed dark stocking feet sticking out one end of the quilt and what appeared to be a head still covered on the other. "Give it a poke with the skillet, Polly," Laura whispered. "Don't come down hard, just a poke. Go ahead."

Before Polly could poke, the form moved, rolling over with arms coming from under the quilt, then the top of a head appeared. Both sisters screamed; Laura dropped the flashlight and Polly the skillet as Belle stood and commenced barking. The form now released from the quilt screamed too. The sisters ran from the room leaving the flashlight and skillet on the floor in the library while they continued to scream huddled together in the kitchen as if in a catatonic stupor with Belle jumping about barked furiously.

"Oh sister, what shall we do?" Polly finally managed to say aloud. But before they had time to think or act, the lighted flashlight was coming towards them with a familiar voice attached to the other end.

"You drop this," Harley said as he approached. "You scare me," he added. "My heart beat fast!"

## CHAPTER SIX

Polly Esther was already in the kitchen frying sausage patties when Laura Alice arrived still in her chenille robe. "Did you go back to sleep last night?" Laura asked. "All I could see when I closed my eyes was the blinding light of that flashlight shining in my face. I thought I was going to have a heart attack."

"After it was all over, I was fine. Did it scare you that it was Harley?"

"It scared me that it was anybody. But, no, I don't think so just because it was him. I don't know how you do it, just turn off things."

"I don't know. Sleep comes easy to me," Polly replied. "I could use some help with breakfast. I'll bet our guest is hungry," Polly added. "We've got a busy day ahead of us. I'll make some coffee."

Harley sauntered in about the same time Laura Alice returned, now dressed for the day. Polly Esther poured coffee for them both. "It smell good in here," Harley said. "It smell like Aunt Effel's breakfast.

Laura Alice started the toast while Polly Esther worked on scrambling the only four eggs she had. As Polly finished the eggs, Laura started squeezing oranges on the glass squeezer atop the wide measuring cup. Harley sat sipping his coffee and eating whatever was put before him. "I forgot to say prayer," he said when he remembered.

"You can say it when you're finished," Laura said. "That way you can remember how good everything tasted and be especially thankful."

"That sound like good idea," Harley said as he kept eating.

"Should I make some oatmeal, sister?" Laura asked as Harley took the last piece of sausage and all the eggs.

"I think we'll be fine," Polly replied, until she saw what remained to be eaten.

Laura Alice opened the cabinet and took out the round Quaker oats box. "Do you want some too?" she asked. Polly nodded yes. Neither sister had eaten yet.

When the last half piece of toast was finished and Harley didn't look as if he wanted more, they sent him home to change his clothes in his apartment before the appointment at the bank. They would meet him there.

"We'll have to get more groceries if he eats here very often," Polly said readying up the dishes. "The eggs are gone, so is the sausage and there's just half a loaf of bread left."

"Poor Ethel fed him every meal," Laura added as she started the water in the dishpan and added some soap.

Laura had been listening as usual for the weather from WOWO, Fort Wayne. She flipped the radio off after she heard there was a chance of rain in the afternoon. "Let's just walk sister," Laura said. "No need to bring the car out to go half a block to the bank. It sounds like we'll be home before it rains. I'll take an umbrella just in case."

"I agree, sister. I hope Harley will get there on time. All he had to do was put on fresh clothes. That shouldn't take long."

The sisters arrived first at the bank and were seated in Warren Haskett's office a few minutes before nine o'clock. A picture of a smiling, now retired, Ralph Stillwell, the bank's past president, greeted them when they looked toward Warren. It was rather unnerving to look in that direction. Instead, with eyes downcast, they sat twisting their hankies in hand and turning every few minutes to look toward the door as if that would make Harley appear sooner. Warren seemed to find enough work on his desk to occupy the time as he waited. When Harley finally arrived, twenty minutes late, to the sister's surprise, he was wearing the same rumpled clothes he had slept in before he went home.

"I sorry. No clothes in drawers. No clothes in closet," Harley said looking toward the sisters as he sat in the chair Warren offered.

"Where are your clothes?" Polly asked looking concerned.

"Clothes dirty," Harley replied.

About this time there was a knock on the door and two others entered, Ralph Stillwell and Bernice Haskett, who was Ralph's daughter and Warren's wife. They took seats as Warren spoke, "I have invited Ralph and Bernice, my wife, to this meeting. This is all a part of the last wishes of Ethel Connelly."

Harley, who was now looking both disheveled and uneasy, stood and moved to stand next to Ralph. Warren got up to move Harley's chair next to Ralph's and resumed his speech.

"My responsibilities as Ethel Connelly's Power of Attorney ceased with her untimely death," Warren began. "However, Ethel had established a trust fund for Harley. That is why I have invited our Trust Department Manager, my wife, Bernice, to attend the meeting." Bernice said nothing and showing no emotion looked ahead to Warren.

"I have also asked Ralph Stillwell, my father-in-law, to attend. Ralph has an interest in Harley which goes back a number of years." That said, he paused, looked at Bernice, and continued. "Harley's mother Janette worked at the same bank as Ralph many years ago in Trenton. Janette was young and found herself with child. Ralph did what he could to help her. Eventually Janette married and moved to Ohio. Her son, Harley, was not accepted by her husband and was placed in a children's home. After Harley's aunt, Ethel Connelly's husband and son died, Ethel gained guardianship of Harley. She moved him to an apartment in her home where he has been for the past year."

Both Laura Alice and Polly Esther were now looking at Ralph and Harley. They wondered how much of what Warren was saying resonated with Harley. He didn't seem offended in what was being said. Again, they were taken back by the obvious friendship between Ralph and Harley.

Then there was Bernice. She hadn't exchanged greeting with the ladies and only established eye contact with her husband. Now she looked down fidgeting with the rings on her fingers.

"The Deerfield State Bank is to be the Durable Power of Attorney for Harley Flynn. A part of the arrangement is a trust established for Harley Flynn by his guardian, his aunt, Ethel Connelly. Bernice Haskett, my wife, is the manager of the Deerfield State Bank Trust Department," Warren went on. "Bernice will now be the manager of that trust. However, there is the need for an appointed person or persons to have access through Bernice to Harley's funds. There will be the need for quick distribution of monies to pay bills related to Harley's living expenses which will be delegated to others in addition to Bernice." Warren kept talking rapidly as if he had rehearsed all that he said and needed to hurry through it.

"Ethel handled all this as Harley's guardian. Now Ethel is gone. Janette Marsh, Harley's mother indicated, when I spoke with her after Ethel's death that she does not want to take on this responsibility." Finally, Warren paused, then looking directly to Laura Alice and Polly Esther, he stated, "Ethel had made known that should anything happen to her, you two ladies should be asked to serve in this relationship with the bank on behalf of Harley. Janette Marsh has agreed as well. Although Bernice would ultimately be in charge of Harley's trust account, you two would be the intermediaries handling his daily needs. There would, of course, be accounting for all funds drawn. Do you have questions about what is involved and what you are being asked to do?"

Laura Alice and Polly Esther looked at each other in surprise. What questions did they have? They didn't know. What had he even said? "I hardly know what to ask," Laura Alice replied while Polly Esther sat mute with wide eyes.

"We are thinking this will facilitate Harley's needs without the appointment of another legal guardian," Warren added. "It will make Harley's trust last longer."

"If you decide to do this," Bernice said, finally looking up toward the sisters, "I will need to meet with you to go over the particulars."

"We need to think on this a while," Polly said. "My sister and I have a business and are quite busy. We don't know how much time this would take. We like Harley, but just need time to think about it."

"How soon would you need to know?" Laura asked.

"I expect we should get things set up within a week. There will be needs which should be taken care of. How about the middle of next week? Say Wednesday? Would that be possible?"

"I think we can decide by then," Laura looked questioningly at Polly who nodded her head in agreement. "Can we call you with questions?"

"Of course; however, Bernice would be the one to speak with," Warren added.

Harley and Ralph sat quietly during the exchanges of the others, Ralph holding Harley's hand on his knee.

"Harley, if you're still going to work today, stop by the shop and I'll get a lunch sack ready for you. I'll make a ham loaf sandwich," Polly said patting Harley on the shoulder as she made her way past his chair. Harley nodded.

"Harley, how about my getting the key to your apartment and getting those dirty clothes washed today," Laura added.

Harley grinned, then responded, "Door unlocked."

The sisters walked home in silence yet there was plenty of self-talk going on for each. Neither knew what she had expected to hear at the bank; in fact, neither had thought about it at all. And what about Ralph? How did he figure in all this?

Laura Alice drew up the shade in the shop and unlocked the door at 10:15 a.m. Polly quickly made and wrapped a ham loaf sandwich in wax paper. She put it along with an apple and some cookies in a brown paper sack in the refrigerator in case Harley came by, which he did shortly thereafter. Polly then went to the shop to relieve Laura Alice who would go two doors north to Harley's apartment with a laundry basket in hand.

Sure enough, the door to Harley's apartment was unlocked. The kitchen she entered certainly hadn't gotten any tidier than what it had been when the sisters had taken the hot dish last week. The burned food was still on a metal pan in the oven. Dishes filled the table, including the empty dish they had taken which now contained dried crusty remains and a spoon slanting inside. All this would have to be attended to later. Now she would gather up the clothes, take them home to wash, and get on with the business of the shop.

The apartment consisted of the kitchen, a small sitting room, bath, and bedroom. Ethel had had workmen from Miller's Lumberyard come in to do the work, the same lumberyard where Harley now worked. Ralph had something to do with the lumberyard, but she wasn't sure just what. Anyway, now she needed to get the clothes.

There were dirty clothes in each room, including an assortment of towels and washcloths on the floor in the bathroom. The bedroom was a mess as well. Tossing the blankets aside, she pulled off the sheets and crammed them onto the already full laundry basket. Picking up a pillow, she pulled off the case, and threw it into the basket, then lifted the last pillow. She noticed blood on the back of the case. Perhaps Harley's nose has bled, she thought. When she pulled off the case, something hard, and wrapped in dried blood soaked tissue fell landing with a thud on the linoleum covered floor. She stooped to look, but didn't want to touch. She looked about for something to scrape away the soiled tissue stuck to the object. There were empty metal hangers in the nearby closet. Using one, she scraped at the paper. There was some writing, but what? Using another hanger to hold the object in one place, she scraped with the other. The tissue was slowly torn away and words became visible as the shape of the object was exposed. It was Ethel's Bavarian whetstone, with the words Deerfield State Bank printed on the side. She dropped the hangers, put a hand to her mouth as if covering her shock and ran through the apartment, out the door and back two doors to the shop. *Lord help us!* She kept repeating to herself as she ran.

A bird's eye view from the rim of the Deerfield water tower one street east of Wally's Barber Shop showed Laura's run back to the shop. Then, within half an hour Marshal Homer Collier's squad car could be seen pulling in front of the sewing shop. That was followed by the view of Homer, Laura Alice, and Polly Esther walking quickly to Harley's apartment two doors north.

Next, the sisters were seen going back to the shop and Marshal Collier with something in hand getting into his squad car. From there, he headed south two blocks toward Miller's

Lumberyard. Finally, Wally could be seen leaving his shop and crossing the street to Sisters' Sewing Shop.

Belle 'woofed' in greeting when Wally entered the door. As usual, Wally bent to scratch behind Belle's ears, as she licked his hand. Rising, he spotted Polly seated at the quilting frame, her head in her hands. "What's goin' on here? I saw the marshal's car,"

"It's too terrible to talk about, but I guess it'll have to come out," she moaned. "Laura found Ethel's whetstone in Harley's apartment." Then, she added, as if she didn't really want to, "There was blood on it."

"Do you reckon it was Ethel's?" Wally asked.

"What else would you think?"

"I suppose they'll check it out. What did Harley have to say?" Wally inquired.

"Marshal Collier was headed toward the lumberyard. I don't know what will become of this. Laura Alice is calling Pastor George," Polly said. She pointed toward Laura with her back to Wally as she talked quietly on the phone at the checkout counter. "She thought he needed to know."

"This doesn't look good for Harley. What would he have had against Ethel? She was takin' care of him."

"I don't know, Wally. I can't believe he hurt her, but how did he get that whetstone? That's what I don't understand. Did he find it somewhere?"

Laura Alice put down the phone, turned and walked to the others. "Pastor George will be in prayer about this," she said. "He doesn't think we should announce all this on the prayer chain. He said we could just say there is an urgent unspoken request. He said it might be sending the message that Harley is guilty, and we shouldn't do that. He said we need to wait and see where this goes. I know he's right, it's just hard to wait."

"How will we know if we've waited long enough? Maybe

we should be doing something now. We're supposed to be takin' care of Harley so to speak," Polly said. "But then, maybe he's the one who hurt Ethel."

"You're supposed to be takin' care of Harley? Who told you that?" Wally asked.

Laura gave a quick summary of the bank meeting in the morning while Wally shook his head in disbelief. "Can you believe that Janette woman?" He finally said. "Pushin' her disabled son off on anybody else she could get to watch over him. Ethel knew what she was like, that's why she had him come here to her house."

"We'll pray and wait. Surely we will get some kind of a sign if we're to do something," Laura said.

"Who'd have thought there'd be such a thing right here in Deerfield," Wally added. "It makes a person wonder what the world's coming to."

"Well, I for one don't think Harley did anything wrong. I don't know how that whetstone got in his pillowcase. He probably found it somewhere, or maybe he knows more than he's tellin'."

About this time the heavens let loose and the rains WOWO had predicted came down with a passion pounding against the shop window to the east. They all stood still looking in that direction. "Do you know what else went wrong this morning?" Laura asked.

"I have no idea," Polly replied.

"Me neither," Wally echoed.

"I left my umbrella at the bank," Laura moaned.

"Oh well, this is only supposed to last for the next two or three days. It's a part of one of those 'nor'easters' that's settled over the east coast," Wally went on to say.

"What's a 'nor'easter' anyway?" Polly asked.

"Well, I don't know much about them fancy weather terms,

but it seems it comes to the east off the ocean and brings rain and lots of wind. It's so strong it can come clear to Indiana. At least that's what I got from the radio," Wally explained.

"How are we supposed to get that laundry done?" Laura questioned.

"Harley can't keep wearin' the same clothes he's been in for who knows how long," Polly added.

"Well, I can get your umbrella for you," Wally said, "but I can't make it stop rainin'.

I suppose you could dry some clothes in your cellar if you need to."

"It's so musty in our cellar, they're likely to smell worse than they did before," Polly said. "We'll figure out something. Ethel has such a nice cellar, but we can't use hers. At least I don't want to. I don't want to go down there since what happened."

"I feel the same way. But her cellar would be the perfect place," Laura said. "She has her washer and even has clothesline down there.

"Well suit yourselves. I was just makin' a suggestion. Anyway, I'll get your umbrella as soon as it clears up a bit. For now I'm goin' to make a dash for my shop," Wally said.

"Here, take this old newspaper to put over your head," Polly said as she sorted through some papers in the magazine rack. Wally accepted the covering and dashed through the door as the rain pelted him and the floor inside the open door of the shop. Both sisters were wiping the spray from their arms when they heard the screech of tires on the wet pavement. They looked through the front window in time to see the tail end of a black car rush past and Wally waving on the sidewalk under the awning in front of his store.

## CHAPTER SEVEN

It rained all night and didn't look very hopeful for a change the next day. The WOWO Weatherman said something about the nor'easter being stuck in place over the east coast bringing moisture from the Atlantic as far as the Midwest.

"Does that mean we're going to have rain until the Atlantic goes dry?" Polly Esther asked tongue in cheek to her sister.

"Gracious me, I hope not," Laura Alice replied. "I've had about enough of this. You know what they say about spring rains bringing the flowers."

"It isn't officially spring yet, but at least it isn't snow. We would surely be in worse shape if it was," Polly added as she finished her toast and coffee.

"Have you seen the paper this morning?" It was Nettie on the phone.

"No, is there something I need to see?" Polly Esther asked.

"I think so, Harley's in jail!"

"What! What does it say?"

"You had better read it yourself. I don't know what it all means, but it's not good. I'm calling the others then I'm coming over," she added before she hung up.

Polly Esther went to the front door and retrieved the damp paper that had been left between the storm and main door. She was opening it as she made her way back to the kitchen scanning the front page as she went. Near the bottom of that page was the caption, 'LOCAL MAN HELD.'

    DEERFIELD, Ind. Harley Flynn, nephew of the late Ethel Connelly of Deerfield, is being held as a material witness by the Trenton County Sheriff's Department. Sheriff Winston Rhodes indicated that he has been made aware of new information related to Mrs. Connelly's sudden death from a fall down the steps to her cellar. Homer Collier, Deerfield Marshal transported Flynn to Trenton where he is being held in the jail until the investigation is complete. No further particulars are being released at this time. Sheriff Rhodes indicated that he would not comment during an ongoing investigation.

    The news hit Polly Esther head on. *What have we done?* She thought. *We called Marshal Collier, now Harley's in jail. What were we thinking? We want the truth to come out about Ethel, but we don't want Harley involved. Maybe the blood was Harley's. They surely would check to see if it was Ethel's. Maybe he hurt himself sharpening something.* The thoughts kept coming over and over.

    The phone was ringing again, but she let it ring. Laura Alice had gone in the rain to get Harley's laundry. She needed to see the paper.

    Why hadn't we checked to see if Harley came home last night? We're supposed to be helping him out. Some fine helpers we've turned out to be. It's a good thing we never married or had children. We'd have left them to fend for themselves. Poor Harley.

    Polly rushed to the back door when she heard Laura banging against it. She stepped aside to let Laura come in as she carried the basket of clothes already wet from the rain. Laura's wet hair was plastered to her head with streams of water running down each cheek and dripping from her nose. "Sister, put that basket down and look at this paper!" Polly shouted trying to tell her the news.

"I don't know how I'm ever going to get this laundry done. There's more left to do in the apartment. What's the matter now?" Laura said while wiping her face with a free hand. "I'll tell you what; it'll take me all day to get this laundry done at the rate I'm going. Then, how am I supposed to dry it? And, how are we supposed to run a business with all this mess?"

"Sister, Harley's in jail! Can you believe that! Marshal Collier had Harley locked up!" Polly blurted out.

"Oh no!" Laura Alice responded sitting down at the kitchen table and taking the paper from Polly. "Why? Does he think Harley hurt Ethel?"

"Just read it," she said handing a kitchen towel to Laura. "It talks about Harley being held as a 'material witness.' What does that mean? Does it sound like he thinks Harley is to blame, does it?" Polly asked.

"I don't know what it means, but we need to find out. I'm sure it must be because of that whetstone. What were we supposed to have done, just ignored the bloody thing?"

They could hear commotion in the shop. Belle was barking her usual greeting as Vesta, Nettie, and Thelma made their soggy ways into the kitchen. Before they were all in place, Wally brought up the rear. Closed umbrellas held in hand continued to drip adding to a growing puddle on the kitchen floor. Vesta waved a folded newspaper and everyone seemed to be talking at once as they crowded into the kitchen.

Laura Alice and Polly Esther looked at each other in utter despair. Laura Alice finally put down the newspaper and stood. When all were looking at her she spoke. "Let's go into the shop and find seats. We need to talk."

The quilting ladies pulled straight back chairs from the work table parking their still dripping umbrellas over the backs. Wally found a seat in with the ladies. Belle found a spot near Polly's feet and looked at Laura as well. Vesta folded her newspaper on her lap and all became quiet.

"We might as well tell you what we know about all this," Laura Alice began. "It's not much, but every day it seems like there's more we don't know.

"I found Ethel's whetstone when I went to get Harley's laundry. It had dried blood on it and was in Harley's pillowcase." There were gasps from the listeners.

"Are you sure it was blood?" Thelma asked.

"How did you know to look in Harley's pillowcase?" Nettie followed.

"It looked like blood to me. I didn't know where to look. I was just trying to do the laundry. I wasn't looking for clues. Harley didn't have any clean clothes and we thought we would help," Laura answered.

"We called Marshal Collier. We didn't know what to do. For all we knew it may have been Harley's blood. We knew for sure that Ethel fell down the steps to the cellar. Was she actually hurt in some other way? Was she pushed?" Polly added. "We still don't know."

"We didn't know Marshal Collier had jailed Harley. We thought he would check the blood on the whetstone to see if it was Ethel's. At least that's what I thought," Polly Esther went on. "Now the paper says Harley's being held as a 'material witness.' We don't even know what that means," she continued.

"A material witness is someone the police think knows something about what happened," Wally added. "It doesn't mean they think Harley did anything wrong. Maybe he did and maybe he didn't. That's what I think it means."

"Was this what that urgent unspoken prayer request was about that we got from the church?" Vesta asked.

"Yes," Laura answered. "Pastor George didn't want us to tell about finding the whetstone in Harley's pillowcase so it wouldn't sound like we thought he was guilty."

"Well, I for one don't think Harley did anything wrong," Vesta said. "That poor boy was suffering at her funeral. He was in pain, I tell you. Did you hear him? Now that sister of Ethel's, that's another case. She didn't seem to care one bit. And that dress... like she was goin' to a party."

"I agree with Vesta," Nettie chimed in. "That sister didn't act like she even liked her own son neither. The way she railed out at him. I couldn't believe it, and right there during the service."

"And what's Ralph Stillwell got to do with all this?" Thelma questioned. "He was acting like he's somebody special to Harley. I didn't even know he knew him."

"There's more to that than we know," Wally added. "Ralph stopped by the barber shop this morning on his way to Trenton. He said he was going to bail Harley out of jail."

"What? Bail Harley out? Can he do that if Harley's being held for questioning so to speak?" Vesta asked.

"Well, I don't know," Wally replied. "I'm just telling you what he told me. I don't even know why he stopped. He seemed very upset and I guess he wanted to tell somebody. Ralph doesn't have a lot of close friends in town. He was always kind of standoffish, you know, bein' the banker did that to him I think."

"Is there anything we should be doing to help Harley?" Nettie asked. "What about Harley's father? He wasn't even with his mother at the funeral."

"While we were talking to Janette, she mentioned something about Harley's father. Do you remember exactly what she said, sister?" Polly asked Laura.

"I remember her saying that her husband wasn't Harley's father and that he had never accepted him because of his disabilities. Do you remember her talking about Harley being in a home of some sort before Ethel brought him here to live with her?" Laura asked.

"Yes, I remember her saying that. I remember something else she said. Something that surprised me," Polly went on. "She said that Harley was just like his father, or something to that effect."

"Yes, I do remember her saying that. I wondered at the time exactly what she meant. Did he have disabilities too, or what else did she mean? Who was she talking about? I don't know what she meant," Laura added.

"Homer Collier's my son-in-law, you know," Thelma chimed in. "I wonder if I could get anything out of Sue Ellen, my daughter. I think he tells her things. It's not like we shouldn't know. After all we just want to help Harley."

"I don't know. They're so closed mouthed about official business. I think they have to swear some oath of secrecy to be a marshal. They keep quiet even when something needs to be told," Vesta expressed. "Now if I got a ticket, everybody in town would know. It seems like if you're guilty of something little it's blabbed, but if it's big they keep it secret. We need to know the big stuff, not the little."

"I for one think we should just keep our wits about us and try to find out the facts. Some might say I'm nosey, but I'm just interested. I want to know if Ethel died from an accident, or if somebody pushed her. If she was pushed on purpose, why? Who would want to hurt Ethel? I'm going to see what I can find out from Sue Ellen," Thelma sat firmly resolved folding her arms across her chest.

"I agree with Thelma," Vesta said. "I think I'll ask Marge

Wilson about Harley. She's the bookkeeper at Miller's Lumberyard where Harley works. She may know a thing or two about Harley. I don't think Harley has a mean streak in him, but I'll bet she knows for sure. It could be that Harley was cryin' so at the funeral because he felt guilty of something. Had you thought about that?"

"I did think of that, but I decided he was really just sad that she died. Or maybe he was sad because he knows something and is afraid to tell? He can hardly talk, you know," Nettie added. "Ethel did a lot for him. I don't think he would have done anything bad to her."

"Wally, I have something I need to ask you," Laura said looking seriously in his direction. "Did you give Ralph the gloves he left here at our place? Remember when I gave them to you?"

Wally sat for a while in thought, then said, "Come to think of it, I don't think I did. I think they're still on the shelf in the barber shop. I was planning to give them to him when he came in. I'll check for sure when I go back over. Is it important?"

"Just wondering," Laura replied keeping her thoughts to herself. *I saw those gloves in Ethel's living room. How did they get there? Did you take them there, Wally?*

"We are a trusting bunch. We have all known each other for such a long time. I don't want to think anyone I know would harm a living soul, and yet, our friend has died and there are questions," Polly said. "Pastor George reminded me that we don't want to plant seeds that somebody or other is guilty without proof. We have to remember that and trust that the Lord will lead us in the right direction."

Hazel Watkins, sewing basket in hand, entered the shop just as the group was breaking up. "I came in here to get some help with this dress I'm making. I can't wait for this rain to stop. Easter's coming. I see that Wally Newton has joined the ladies quilting group. I'll have to tell Frank about this. What do you have to say for yourself, Wally?"

Wally stood mute for a while, then responded. "Hazel, you've been makin' too many crazy quilts. I'm wishin' these ladies a happy Easter in advance. You can tell Frank what a gentleman I am."

"Yes, and Wally's thinking about getting a television set for the barber shop," Vesta quickly added. "That's so isn't it, Wally? My Karl said you're thinkin' about it."

"I reckon I have been thinkin' about it. They say them political conventions are gonna be aired this summer. We're gonna get us a new President and I'd sure like to see what goes on. That appliance store in Trenton has a television set in their window. I'm thinking about it, just thinking mind you. See you ladies later." Wally made his exit, thankful that Vesta had changed the subject. Hazel didn't need in on their conversation.

"Say," Hazel began after the others were getting up to leave, "What do you ladies know about what was in the paper today, about that Harley fella? He lives right near you."

"Hazel, we don't know much. We are all anxious about it. I'm sure Marshall Collier is checkin' out everything," Polly replied.

The rain was still coming down as Polly helped Hazel Watkins pin and baste the collar onto the dress she was making for Easter. When that was done, covering her head and sewing project with a raincoat, she dashed from the shop. During the whole time Polly worked with Hazel, Laura Alice quietly sat looking out the window at the rain as if in thought.

When the sisters were finally alone, Laura made a bold statement she never thought she would bring herself to say, "Sister, I have just decided on something I've been thinking about, but tried to put aside. I am going to take Harley's laundry back to Ethel's house, to her basement no less. I might as well use that nice washer she has right there in her basement and hang the clothes up right there. She has clotheslines and pins and is best set up to dry inside. There isn't any reason why I can't do that. The clothes would be right there and we wouldn't have to worry about how we would dry them."

"Sister, are you sure you would feel all right about doing that?" Polly questioned.

"It's foolishness not to feel all right. I'll just do it. If I get them washed, yet today, they'll surely be dry by tomorrow. And I won't worry about ironing anything, except maybe the shirts," Laura added. "At least Harley will have clean clothes."

"Do you want me to help you, sister?" Polly asked.

"No you stay here. It's two hours until closing time. I can get a lot done in two hours."

"Wear that old raincoat of father's. I know where it is," Polly said rushing to get it.

Laura, who had been sitting in wet clothes, put on dry ones. After Polly produced the old raincoat, she began wiping the cobwebs from the inside and out. Even though the coat smelled musty like the basement of their house, it would keep Laura dry as she went again to Ethel's.

Once more she carried the basket with wet dirty clothes through the B.P.O.E. parking lot to Ethel's lawn, and made her way up the apartment steps. Again, she entered Harley's apartment, this time going to the door, in the kitchen, that led to the basement. She had never entered the basement from this side.

She held the basket with her right hand against the side of the stairwell to her left while searching with her left hand for a switch. Soon a single bulb glowed in the center of the cellar ceiling. Although it was midafternoon, the basement was still dim with the single bulb and scant light coming through four small ground level windows to the outside. It would take a while until her eyes began to see things more clearly.

Laura had been in this basement a few times in the past when Ethel had shown her the new washer and another time when she had shown Laura the bounty of canning she had done.

Ball jars still lined the shelves on the long side of the cellar with a colorful variety of vegetables preserved by Ethel. Laura spotted the grape juice jars remembering how Ethel contributed each year at Easter for the Communion service at church. Who would do it this year? She could feel the presence of her dear friend through the work of her hands.

She could see the steps on the other side of the room coming from Ethel's house. Beneath them would be where Ethel fell. She consciously didn't want to look at them closely, making herself look elsewhere.

The washer and rinse tubs were against the far wall to the left near the water faucets, water heater and drain. Laura carried her load in that direction. This would be all right. It would be the easiest thing to do. She began to sort the clothes in piles by colors on the floor. She filled the wash tub with hot water and added soap from the box on the shelf above the washer. She put in the white things and started the motion of the washer. Then she remembered the things still in Harley's apartment. She should get them as well.

She wasn't sure when the fear began. The first trip through the apartment to the basement had been bold without the slightest hint of doubt. But, sometime between that time, being in the basement and returning to search in Harley's apartment, doubt had crept in. Was it the memory of finding the bloody whetstone? What if someone else had planted it there? Others surely had access to Harley's apartment the same as she. Harley seldom locked the door. What else might she find? Who else may have been there? Who may be waiting upstairs in one of the rooms? She couldn't bring herself to go through the rooms again. She would wash only what she had sorted on the floor and leave as soon as she could. She was halfway up the steps when she turned, looked about and returned to the washer.

She worked quickly to run each load in the hot sudsy water in the washer, then through the wringer into the rinse water. Finally each load went through the wringer one last time to remove excess water before they were hung. Ethel's clothes pin bag, which she had made, still hung filled with wooden pins. As she anchored each article of clothing with the pins, she could see through the small windows the sky beginning to look orange. Evening was coming soon and it would be dark. She wanted to be home before then.

The clothes were finally all hanging, the rinse water drained, and the washer draining in progress when Laura heard someone stepping upstairs in Ethel's side of the house. At first she thought it was just her imagination. So far as she knew, Harley was still in jail. Then it was for real, not imagination. The steps were firm and becoming more pronounced. She stood paralyzed as the water continued to drain from the washer and the door through which Ethel had fallen opened with new light coming from above. There was no time to run, or place to hide, as the shoes of a man and now his legs appeared to be coming slowly down the steps.

"What's going on down here?" a voice shouted. The man was fully in sight now, with a gun drawn. "What the. . . ?" his voice trailed off as he saw who it was.

"It's me, Marshal," Laura finally said leaning against the now drained washer to keep from falling.

She covered her face and started wailing, her emotions

finding release. The marshal put away his gun and put an arm about her.

"What are you doing here, Miss Laura," Marshal Collier asked.

"I'm trying to do some laundry for Harley," she sobbed. "I didn't have any place to hang them at our house."

"Did you get done?" the marshal asked, smiling.

"Yes, how did you know I was here?" Laura asked.

"Skipper saw the basement light when he was on his paper route. He told me about it. I thought I'd take a look.

"You were takin' a chance coming in here like this. How did you get in?"

"I came through Harley's apartment. He's not home, you know. But Wally said Ralph is planning to bail him out. Is that so?"

"We'll find out about that tomorrow. You need to get home now. It's getting dark out. You don't come over here anymore like this. You hear me. I don't want anything to happen to you. That apartment needs to be locked."

"What should I do about the clothes?" Laura asked.

"They're clean aren't they?"

"Well, yes."

"Just let them hang here. If Harley gets home, they'll be ready for him," Marshal Collier finally said.

Laura Alice felt plainly foolish as the marshal escorted her up the steps, turned off the cellar light, and then walked her home. She felt even more foolish when he told Polly Esther to see that neither she nor her sister do any more laundry in Ethel's basement. After the marshal left, Polly made a pot of tea for them both. "We need something to calm us down, sister," Polly said. "At least you got the laundry done."

After a quiet supper of potato soup and biscuits, the sisters once more sat at the quilting frame working on a Double-Wedding-Ring quilt. Their schedule for getting that quilt ready by June had been sorely disrupted of late.

"Oh drat," Polly exclaimed aloud. "I stuck myself and there's a drop of blood right on that white piece. Don't you know what happens when you've been upset about something?"

"Don't touch anything until I get back," Laura said heading toward the kitchen. She quickly returned with a bottle of white vinegar and a clean cloth. "Here, let me blot that stain with this vinegar. It should take it off since it's not set. Go get yourself a band-aide for that finger," she said as she started blotting.

Polly returned to find the stain completely gone. "Now I can't find where I left off. It's like they say, 'haste makes waste.' I need to settle down, quit hurrying and get my mind settled."

"I know," Laura said. "We go along in our usual way, and then everything gets out of whack. First Ethel died, the funeral, that bloody whetstone, now Harley in jail."

"I hate to say it, Sister, but it all seems to have gone wrong since we started the zodiac sampler."

"Are you saying 'I told you so'?" Laura asked.

"I'm not saying that. I'm just saying that all this has happened since we started those blocks. Do you realize that we start a new block at the quilters club this Thursday? Aries runs from March 21st and goes to April 19th. I don't think anyone has a birthday in that sign."

"Are you sure? It seems like something I heard lately reminded me of that sign," Laura questioned.

"I'm thinking the same. Who was it? It's terrible when we start thinking of birthdays by a zodiac sign."

"I know!" Laura Alice blurted. "It was at the funeral home. Janette said that Harley would soon be thirty. His birthday is on April first."

"Oh yes, I remember that. I was thinking it was sad that his birthday would be then," Polly said. "It seems like some people get all the bad breaks right from the start."

"You can say that. Having Janette as his mother was his first bad break. I wonder if Ralph Stillwell will be able to get Harley out of jail. What will happen if he can't? It's all so unsettling."

The next day was delightfully calm, and Polly Ester and Laura Alice closed the shop promptly at 5:00 p.m. Polly made pancakes and stewed apples for supper while she listened to Lowell Thomas on the radio. By 6:30 Wally had arrived with Laura Alice's umbrella she had left at the bank and inquired about the state of Harley's laundry.

Polly Esther had begun the tale of Laura's laundry experience, when Laura interrupted.

"Wally, would you go with us over to the apartment?"

"Sister, what are you thinking?" Polly interrupted this time. "Do you remember what the marshal said? You are not to go over there and do laundry again. And don't include me in your plans."

"I know, I've already done the laundry. I won't do that again. I just want to take the clothes down and fold them," Laura began. 'And besides, we need to get those dishes washed in the kitchen and straighten up things."

"Miss Laura," Wally said as he chuckled, "You are hopeless. You are a do-gooder."

"Just leave well enough alone," Polly added. "You have done enough. What will the marshal say if he finds you over there again."

"We could get this done before he would notice. He wouldn't think we would be over there again so soon. It wouldn't take long. If we all three went, we could get the clothes down, folded, the bed made, the dishes done and out of there in no time.

What do you say?"

"If you're bound to go, I'll go with you," Wally finally said. "What about you, Miss Polly. We could get things done faster if you went too."

"If we get arrested, I will say you two made me," Polly said. "Let's go before it gets any darker. . . one hour, then I'm coming home."

The evening was calm as the threesome made it past the B.P.O.E. parking lot now in view of Ethel's house. As they walked, a familiar green Studebaker pulled in front of Ethel's house. Doors slammed and two familiar people emerged carrying suitcases.

"Ralph, Harley!" Wally yelled and the men looked up. They stood in place as the others joined them. "Glad to see you Harley," Wally said. "We've got clean laundry for you, Harley. It's in the basement."

"We've been worried about you, Harley," Laura said.

"Are you all right?" Polly asked, now touching Harley's arm.

"I all right," Harley said. "I hungry."

"I'm Harley's new guardian," Ralph spoke up. "I saw my attorney today," he added.

"I'll be staying here in Ethel's house for a while. Harley can stay in his apartment."

"Have you eaten any supper?" Polly asked.

"No," Ralph replied. "We'll find something."

"You'll find something in our kitchen once you put those suitcases down," Polly said. "I've made pancakes for supper."

"I like pancakes," Harley added. The suitcases, which were Ralph's, were taken into the house, then all started back to the sisters' kitchen.

Wally, Ralph and Harley settled in the library while Polly Esther hurriedly mixed up more pancake batter and Laura Alice went to their cellar to get two more quarts of stewed apples.

Soon the sweet scent of the food, and the clatter of tableware filled the kitchen as Harley, Ralph, and, yes, Wally too, all ate their fill of pancakes and stewed apples.

Harley and Ralph could tend to the dried laundry themselves and wash the dirty dishes back in the apartment.

## CHAPTER EIGHT

The groundhog had not seen his shadow in February and sure enough, spring seemed to be coming early this year in spite of the deluge of rain with the nor'easter in late March. It was just a little over three weeks until Easter. Robins were busy with nests, buds were beginning to swell on shrubs and trees, and each day was light a bit longer. Since the evening when Ralph brought Harley home from jail nothing had been seen or heard from them even though both were occupants of Ethel's house two doors north.

Nettie, Vesta, and Thelma all made their way into the shop carrying their sewing baskets this Thursday for Sampler Club. The usual seating pattern was soon established around the work table before baskets were opened and fabric removed. This was the final day for the old block, the Pisces pattern. There would be 'show and tell' for the old and time to cut out the new pieces for Aries. The extra block Vesta had made from Ethel's fabric was shown as well, and everyone agreed that Ethel would be pleased.

"I guess you all know by now that Harley's out of jail," Laura said. "He's staying over there in his apartment, and Ralph Stillwell is staying up front in Ethel's house. Can you imagine that? We still don't know what's going on with Ralph and Harley. Ralph said he's Harley's new guardian. He said he saw his attorney."

"Does it mean that Harley didn't hurt Ethel if they let him out?" Nettie asked.

"I don't know," Laura said. "I don't think they would let him out if they thought he had.

"Vesta, did you talk to Marge Wilson at the lumberyard about Harley?"

"Yes, I sure did. She said Harley wouldn't hurt anybody, not even if he needed to. He mostly sweeps floors and dusts around the displays. She said something else that was interesting. She said that Ralph Stillwell sends a check each month to pay Harley's salary. His pay doesn't come from Mr. Miller, the lumberyard owner."

"Well, I'll be," Thelma said. "I guess she should know. She's the bookkeeper."

"Why do you suppose he does that? Is he related to Harley somehow?" Nettie asked.

"I don't know, but I'd sure like to find out," Vesta said, and everyone agreed.

Thelma began to squirm in her chair and said she had found out a few things they may not want to hear. "Sue Ellen said Homer told her told her that Ethel had some injuries that didn't seem like they came from a fall."

"Oh dear, I wonder what kind of injuries?" Vesta asked.

"Well, she said Homer finally told her they were injuries you would likely get defending yourself," Thelma responded. "Homer said there were cuts on her chest, long cuts on the backs of her forearms, and on the palms of her hands."

"Oh no, poor Ethel! We don't know the half of what she went through," Nettie voiced and the others agreed.

"Could the injuries have come from that whetstone striking her?" Nettie continued.

"I suppose they think it could have been. Maybe that's why

they jailed Harley," Vesta said. "I'm sure they tested the blood to see if it was hers."

"Sue Ellen said that Homer told her there was bruising on her back which the coroner thought was probably caused by the fall before she hit her head on the concrete floor." Thelma began slowly after she had sat quietly with her head down for a while, "Her neck was broken."

There were moans and sorrowful expressions as Thelma continued. "I hate to tell you all this. It makes it so bad for Ethel. I hate to think what she went through. Why did this happen to Ethel? Nothing from the house had been taken as far as they know."

"Why is Ralph staying at Ethel's? He has that big house he and Irma lived in on past the church," Vesta said.

"I think his son-in-law and daughter moved in there with him when they came here from Trenton. He's at the bank you know. . . gave us those whetstones. What's his name?" Nettie asked.

"Warren Haskett is his name and his wife, Ralph's daughter works at the bank too. She has to do with the trust department. Her name is Bernice," Polly added. "We met her at a meeting we went to about a trust fund for Harley. I don't think she lived here when she was growing up. I think she went to some fancy school somewhere. You know how Irma, Ralph's wife was. Nothing around here was good enough for her. I shouldn't say that, but that was how it seemed to me."

"I only remember seeing her a couple times," Vesta added. "I got that impression too."

"We best get busy cutting the new block pieces or we won't be ready to sew next week, "Laura reminded the ladies. "No one in our group has a birthday for the next sign, but," she paused, "Harley does. He's going to be thirty. Can you imagine that? He seems much younger. Maybe we can each send him a card. I doubt that he will get much else."

"Send him a card? I don't know about that. Maybe he's the one that hurt Ethel, someone did. I'll bet you anything Harley knows more about it than he's tellin'," Thelma said.

"You know he has a problem talkin'. Maybe he can't find the words to talk about it. You saw him at the funeral. He can't just say things like most people can," Nettie went on.

"And Ralph too, what does he know about what went on? Why is he staying with Harley? There's something Ralph's not talking about either," Vesta added.

"We all know that Ethel kept secrets for us. We could tell her anything and she'd never gossip. She was likely keeping secrets for others too. Maybe that's why she was hurt?" Nettie said.

"If she was keeping secrets, they were dangerous ones, I would say," Thelma went on.

Before the Sampler Club left, they all agreed not to send cards to Harley. Polly wanted to make cupcakes for him, but the others cautioned. In case he hurt Ethel, it wouldn't be a good idea to give him cards or cupcakes.

\* \* \*

"How about we play Scrabble tonight?" Wally was asking. "I guess I'm looking for words. I've been thinking about words all day."

"Words! Now that sounds strange," Polly responded.

It was Friday evening. The Barber Shop and Emporium had closed nearly two hours ago as had Sisters' Sewing Shop. Polly wanted to make a rhubarb pie to serve tonight, but she was rushing the season. The rhubarb wasn't up yet even though she could see that it had survived the winter and was beginning to push up near the back door. Instead, she baked a lemon meringue pie which might satisfy the tart taste that teased her taste buds. The pie with crusty, perfectly browned swirls of meringue on top sat in inviting readiness on the kitchen counter.

"What kind of words are you trying to find?" Laura Alice inquired, "Something in particular?"

"I've been talkin' to Ralph this week. Or rather, I've been listenin' to Ralph. He's been doin' the talkin'. That man has a lot to tell, I'm tellin' you!

"And another thing," he said, handing over a pair of brown leather gloves with the monogram RHS on the cuff, "I keep forgetting to give these to Ralph. The winter's almost over and they're still on my shelf. I thought maybe you could get them to him faster than me."

Laura, with a puzzled expression on her face, took the gloves, carefully looking at the monograms before lifting them to whiff the scent of Old Spice. "We haven't seen much of Ralph, but maybe we will before long. I'll try to get them to him." *What is the story of these gloves? Our house, Ethel's house, Wally's shop, now our house?* She thought as she put the gloves once again on the hall table.

"Come on to the library," Polly said. "I think I can find that Scrabble game. We've got lemon meringue pie for later. I hope you like that."

"I like anything with the last name of pie," Wally replied. "Do I have to wait until later? I'm ready for pie now."

"I'll get the Scrabble game; Polly, you cut the pie. That sounds good to me too," Laura said as she opened the library closet door revealing shelves of stored games.

Situated at the game table, with pie at hand, the game took on a secondary role. Wally was plainly more interested in eating and talking. "That was a mighty small piece of pie, Miss Polly. Do you reckon I could have a second?" he said as he scraped the last of the lemony custard from the plate and drained the last of his coffee.

Laura turned the Scrabble tiles over in readiness to begin the game while Wally ate. "If you ever decide to sell pies in the shop, I'd like one of this kind," Wally said, finishing his second piece as well the seconds of coffee. "That was delicious," he said patting his stomach.

"Now about Ralph," he began, "That man's been in torment. He's relivin' things he's held onto for years. He's stayin' over there at Ethel's place you know."

"Why is he staying there, anyway?" Laura asked. "He's got that big house. What's the matter with that?"

"It's a long story and it's not over yet. His daughter, Bernice, and her husband, Warren moved in there with him when they came back to town. Warren's at the bank, you know. Ralph thought that would work out fine since he was in that big house by himself. Well, it hasn't worked out that way. Instead of them living with Ralph, He says it's like they took over the whole house and he's living with them. They moved most of Ralph's personal things into one bedroom and he was sleepin' in another. They took over the rest of the house. Anyway, Ralph's feelin' cramped."

"I'm sure it takes a while to get used to new arrangements," Polly said.

"Well, it's not just that. Ralph wanted to move Harley in there with them, when he got him out of jail. But, they said no. Bernice said it was a slur on her mother's memory."

"What did that have to do with her mother's memory?" Laura asked. "This doesn't make sense. Why did Ralph bail Harley out anyway? I'm glad he did, but why?"

"This all goes back a long way. Ralph and Irma lived in Trenton when they were first married. Ralph worked at the bank there. He became an officer after a while. Well, it seems that Janette Flynn, Ethel's sister started working there. You know who she is.

"Yes, we met Janette."

"Well, Janette wasn't like Ethel at all. She was younger than Ethel and lived with Ethel and her husband at the time. They lived in Trenton back then too. Janette had a way about her. Some of the words I've been tryin' to find have to do with her. The words that come to mind aren't the kind I want to use around ladies," he said, looking down and fingering the Scrabble tiles.

"We talked with Janette at the funeral. She seemed 'flighty' and not at all interested in Harley," Polly said.

"She wanted us to help with Harley and had already talked with Warren Haskett about it, then she was gone," Laura added.

"Ralph says that Janette uses people. He said she uses them to get what she wants, then moves on. He said she did that to him," Wally said.

"She used Ralph? What did she do to him?" Polly inquired.

"This was the part Ralph had a hard time talkin' about. He said Janette 'vamped' him," Wally said. All was quiet as the sisters looked at each other then back to Wally.

"She did what?" Polly asked.

"I don't understand either," Laura added.

"V-A-M-P-E-D," Wally spelled the word and sat mute, still looking down.

"She vamped him in his office a couple of times and once in the vault! Can you imagine?" Wally went on, his voice rising with emotion. "Ralph had never had anyone act that way to him before. He was the victim, so he says."

"Oh, dear me," Laura said. "I think I understand."

"Gracious, didn't he have any choice?" Polly added demurely.

"Well anyway, it wasn't long before Ralph knew he was into something that was gonna be a big problem for him. Janette was gettin' more bold at the bank, and there was Irma at home," Wally went on. "He had to do somethin.'"

"What did he do?" the sisters asked looking questioningly to Wally.

"He did the only thing he could think of. He needed to get away," he paused. "He joined the Army."

"Joined the Army!" the sisters said in unison.

"Yes, Irma thought he was being patriotic, but he had other reasons."

"Where did he go? How long was he gone?" Polly Esther and Laura Alice were asking.

"He said he was gone for two years. During that time he was down along the southern border in New Mexico and Arizona. There was some trouble goin' on there and troops had been sent. Ralph was there. He said it was so blazin' hot, he felt like he'd been sent to hell. Excuse me ladies me for saying that."

"What happened when he came back?" Laura asked and Polly nodded her eagerness to know.

"When he came back, he met his daughter, Bernice. Irma had given birth eight months after he had left. He resumed his position at the bank and life went on."

"What about Janette?" Polly asked.

"Janette had left. She had met an insurance salesman, that had called on Ethel and Cecil, got married, and moved to Ohio. Ralph didn't know it then, but Janette also was going to have a child. In fact she had twins, two boys. His children he says. They were born just a few weeks before Bernice. She named one child Harley after Ralph's middle name, Harlan and the other Quinton. He doesn't know why.

"She hadn't told her new husband that she was expecting, but he soon found out. She was beginnin' to blossom. After the boys were born, she gave Quinton to Ethel and her husband who adopted him. She was planning to keep Harley, but her husband had other plans. There was a struggle of some kind with her husband and the child was dropped. He spent time in the hospital, and was left with permanent brain injuries. Her husband refused to allow the child to come home. Janette put Harley in a home for disabled children until Ethel got him out after Quinton died."

"Ralph didn't know about the children?" Laura asked.

"No, Ralph didn't know about them for years. In fact it wasn't until he moved to Deerfield years later. He met Ethel and Cecil through the bank. One thing led to another and the link to Janette was uncovered."

"Well, I'll be. All those years, then the connection. I wonder how that happened?" Laura asked.

"It came about through the name of Flynn. Ethel had used that name as her second name at the bank. Ralph mentioned that he had once known someone by that name in Trenton and the connection came out. Then after Cecil and Quinton had died, Ethel moved Harley here to Deerfield, Ralph uncovered more of the truth and had the evidence right before him. Irma died shortly after that. She never knew about the boys."

"So that's why Ralph has been so protective of Harley. Do Bernice and Warren know about all this?" Polly asked.

"It seems they're finding out, and Bernice is furious. She refuses to accept Harley as a half-brother. She says none of it's true. That's why Ralph is staying at Ethel's. I don't know what's going to happen. It's not over by a long shot," Wally said still fingering the tiles before him. "If you ladies don't mind, I'd just as soon go home. I don't really feel like playing a game."

"Me neither," said Polly.

"Nor me," Laura added.

"Next week is Harley's birthday," Polly said. "I wonder if Ralph knows."

"I'll tell him," Wally said as he stood and dusted the pie crust crumbs from his belly. "What day?"

"April 1st," Polly answered.

"Well, I'll be. Don't that take all!" Wally said. "That'll be a reminder to Ralph. Poor Harley." Wally said, shaking his head. "I wonder if Quinton knew who his mother was and that he had a twin brother."

Wally had gone. Polly carried the pie plates and silverware to the kitchen, took out the dishpan and commenced running the hot water. Laura picked up the Scrabble pieces, put the box back in the closet and joined Polly in the kitchen.

"Sister, sometimes I'm glad we didn't mingle much. You know what I mean," Polly said as she washed the pie plates and silverware.

"I know what you mean, sister," Laura responded. "It all sounds so complicated. Imagine 'vamping' someone. I would be so embarrassed."

"It's too shameful to even think about," Polly said. "No wonder we didn't get married. We never tried to vamp anyone. I don't think we knew how."

The dishes were done and the remains of the pie in the refrigerator; the sisters walked to the library. It was too early for bed, and they needed time to reflect, to be calm. Wally had told them too much to be digested all at once. Polly examined a few books from the many choices, returning each to the shelf until she settled on *The Grapes of Wrath*. Laura chose *Gone with the Wind*. She had never made it all the way through. When things were overwhelming, she more than once had tried to lose herself in the exploits of Scarlet O'Hara. Maybe it was easier to think on the problems of characters in a book than to think of the ones closer to home. This was such a time. Belle walked about the chair where Wally had sat nibbling what remained of the crumbs.

"Wally said, 'This story's not over yet,'" Laura restated. "I believe he's right about that."

"Do you think any of what Wally told us has to do with Ethel dying?" Polly finally asked Laura, as she was supposed to be reading.

"I'm wondering the same," Laura replied, laying her book aside.

## CHAPTER NINE

"Sister, we haven't heard a thing from Harley and Ralph," Polly Ester said as the two worked at the quilting frame Tuesday evening. "Do you think we're still supposed to be helping with Harley's finances?" The clock ticked off three or four minutes before Laura Alice responded.

"Since Ralph is the guardian all that arrangement is probably off. What do you think?"

"Maybe it is and maybe it's not. I don't know. We should find out," Polly said. "We told Warren and Bernice that we would let them know by the middle of this week whether or not we would help Harley. I think we should talk to them and find out what's what. It never hurts to make things clear."

"You're right, sister. I was assuming it was off, but we should be sure. Tomorrow is Wednesday. One of us could go to the bank and talk to them."

"If they want us to help him, should we? We haven't even talked about it since Wally told us Ralph was guardian," Polly said.

"You know we have to help him if they still need us. There doesn't seem to be anyone else they're asking. I don't think we'll be needed though. Ralph's the banker. He could surely take care of Harley's finances," Laura added. "Would you feel all right about going to the bank tomorrow to find out what's going on? If we both go, we'd have to close the store."

"I was hoping you would go. I'm not very good at speaking up like you are," Polly responded.

"You do all right," Laura said.

"Not when I'm by myself. I can when you're with me, but somebody needs to stay here at the shop anyway."

"All right, I'll go. I don't think there'll be much to it. They'll just tell me that we aren't needed," Laura said.

The clock struck nine and Polly parked her needle and took off her thimble. "I'll take Belle out then I'm going to bed. I've had enough for today. Sometimes I feel like I'm one of them wind-up toys doing the same thing every day."

Laura Alice finished the block she was working on, parked her needle and thimble before holding the palms of her hands over her burning eyes. My eyes are feeling the strain of this close work more and more. I should get them checked.

\* \* \*

"My sister and I thought we should get back with you about helping Harley with his finances. We said we'd let you know," Laura said as she was seated in Bernice Haskett's office at the Deerfield State Bank. "We didn't figure you would need us now that your father is Harley's guardian."

At the last remark, Bernice suddenly sat up rigid in her seat as her expression froze in place, "Who told you that!" she demanded.

"Well, Wally Newton, Ralph's friend, told us. That's so isn't it?"

"It certainly is not!" Bernice exclaimed. "My father is having some personal problems right now and he is not able to serve as anyone's guardian. I was going to call you and your sister today to see if you had decided to work with the bank on Harley's behalf."

Laura Alice was now adjusting herself in the chair which

suddenly felt harder than when she first sat down. "Polly Esther and I want to help Harley. We just didn't think we would be needed. Will he have a guardian?"

"As my husband had said at our last meeting, we think the bank can serve Harley's needs without the need for a guardian," Bernice said. "Perhaps his mother will make other living arrangements for him in the near future. He may be moving from our community soon."

"His mother didn't seem too eager to help him, from what I saw," Laura added. "His Aunt Ethel was the one who took care of him, but your father seems to want to help him now."

"My father didn't even know Harley existed until that Connelly woman led him to believe he had some responsibility. She led him to believe things that aren't true," Bernice said, her eyes blazing as she looked directly at Laura.

Laura Alice sat mute. It didn't seem like a good time to mention what Wally had told them about Ralph and Janette at the bank in Trenton years ago. It was obvious that Bernice would not have welcomed that conversation. "If you still need Polly Esther and me to help with Harley's finances, we're willing," Laura finally said.

The rest of the conversation centered on instructing Laura about what the bank expected of them. She left after having signed a form which authorized her to sign checks on Harley's behalf as well as receiving a checkbook. Polly Esther would need to come by the bank to authorize her signature on a check for Harley too unless they wanted only Laura to sign. The sisters would need to talk about that. They would also need to talk about much more, namely, Bernice. She certainly wasn't about to accept Harley as anything but a bank client.

Laura Alice headed south, walking along the east side of the block feeling like she had been run over by a truck. That woman, Bernice, what to make of her? How can wanting to help Harley make me feel like I'm a terrible person? Is Ralph not mentally able to help Harley? 'That Connelly woman,' what to make of that? I feel like we're in the middle of a fight, but why? What have we gotten into?

Laura was just about to cross the street when, "Hello down there," came a voice loud and clear from above. Immediately Laura Alice turned, looking up to her left and shielding her eyes from the bright sky above. There were two figures on the top of the building, Wally's building. One figure was larger than the other with a rounded mid-section while the other was half a head shorter and thin. Her eyes couldn't quite make out who it was until she heard the voice again. "It's us, Wally and Harley." She could make out one of them waving while the other held a contraption of some sort.

"What are you doing up there?" she called back still shielding her eyes.

"Television antenna!" Wally yelled. "It has to go up here somehow."

"Be careful," Laura added. "Don't get too close to the edge."

"We're fine. Harley's helpin' me get this dang thing put up here. Ralph's in the barber shop. Could you check with him to see if we're connected?" Wally yelled.

Harley waved to Laura. She returned his wave and added, "You be careful too, Harley." She ducked into the barber shop to see Ralph positioned before a brightly lit, but fuzzy television screen.

"What's it supposed to look like?" Laura questioned Ralph.

"There's supposed to be pictures of people, that's what," Ralph replied. "We'll be lucky if we can figure out how to make this thing work," Ralph said as he twisted dials back and forth.

"Wally wants to know if it's hooked up," Laura said.

"I reckon it is? At least something happened a while ago. I got a fuzzy picture. I'll go up and tell him what it looks like,"

Ralph said before heading to the back of the shop and the stairs.

Inside the shop across the street, Polly was measuring fabric while two ladies waited at the cutting table. Agnes Fritz was seated nearby looking through patterns. All the excitement from the bank and the rooftop across the street would have to wait. There was business at hand.

The day continued to be busy with customers planning last minute sewing projects before Easter. Each sister took a quick lunch break while the other stayed in the shop. Then, came an afternoon lull before the shop doors were locked, the 'closed' sign turned out, and the blind pulled down. "What a whirlwind!" Laura exclaimed. "Now to clean up the remains," she added as she started to fasten loose ends of fabric bolts and returned them to shelves. "We haven't had a minute to catch our breath."

"I've been wondering all day what you found out at the bank," Polly said as she straightened the patterns.

"Before we talk about that, I want you to look out the front door," Laura said, walking to the door and turning the safety lock. "Look on top of Wally's place."

The sisters stepped just outside the door. "Now look up," Laura continued.

"We'll I'll be. He did it. He got that television set and we've got an antenna right across the street from us, right here in Deerfield," Polly Esther said.

"Wally and Harley were on the roof when I came from the bank. It looks like they got the antenna up. I hope it won't fall over or blow away. That'll be the talk in the barber shop, even the whole town for that matter," Laura said as they stepped back inside and again locked the door.

"Let's sit a while so I can tell you about the bank," Laura said as they walked to the kitchen.

"Let me get this tuna casserole started while you talk," Polly said. "You know I can't sit still while supper's waitin.'"

"I'll set the table while I'm talking," Laura said, relaying the events at the bank while they hustled about the kitchen.

"Sister, I just had an idea," Polly said. "I think I should make a little extra tuna casserole, put it in another dish and take it to Harley and Ralph. What do you think?"

"I agree. I'll see if we've got another can of tuna. Do we have some extra noodles to cook?" Laura asked.

"I'll just finish the rest of this package of noodles. I hadn't used them all."

"Another thing, I could take those gloves of Ralph's back to him. I still want to know how those gloves were at Ethel's while Wally supposedly had them."

Before long the sisters had baked the casserole, prepared a side dish of peas and carrots, and put some oatmeal cookies in a bag to take two doors to the north. Laura got the gloves with the RHS embroidered on the cuffs; and between them, they carried the picnic basket with the food covered with tea towels.

"Which door should we go to?" Polly asked as they got past the B.P.O.E. "Ralph's car is still out front. Maybe they're mostly in Ethel's place. Let's go to the front door."

It didn't take long for Ralph to open the door, looking somewhat puzzled at seeing the ladies. Harley was standing close beside. "I thought maybe it was Bernice," Ralph said.

"It's just us," Laura said. "Polly and I made a little extra supper for you this evening. I hope you haven't eaten yet."

"Well, no. We haven't," Ralph said. "I'm not much of a cook. We've been having a lot of scrambled eggs and toast lately."

"He burn toast," Harley said, snickering, Ralph didn't respond.

"Wally told us you were both staying here. Can I take this to the kitchen?" Polly said holding the basket forward. Ralph didn't respond.

"I've got some gloves for you," Laura said while Polly stayed in place. "I think these are yours," she said handing the gloves to Ralph. She turned to see the similar pair still on the side table where she had seen them earlier. There were indeed two pairs of embroidered gloves.

"You left these at our house when you and Wally came to play games. I see there's another pair just like these," she said picking up the pair from the table.

"Oh yes," Ralph answered. "Ethel was so good to put my initials on my gloves so I wouldn't lose them, but it didn't seem to help. Bernice gives me brown leather gloves for Christmas every year. She knows I often lose them. A year ago I left a pair at Ethel's; she put my initials on them. She was working on a pair from this past year. I hadn't even got them yet. I didn't see them on the table. Ethel was a good woman," Ralph added.

"Ralph, could we talk a bit?" Laura asked looking at him seriously.

"I suppose so," Ralph said. "I don't have much to talk about."

"I was at the bank today," Laura began. "You remember when Warren and Bernice asked us sisters if we would help Harley with his finances."

"Yes, I remember that," Ralph answered.

"I went back today to see if the bank still wanted us to do that. We thought maybe things had changed since then. I talked with Bernice," Laura continued.

"What did she say?" Ralph quickly asked.

"Well, Wally told us that you were going to be Harley's guardian so we figured that you would take care of his finances, you being a banker and all," Polly added.

"What did she say?" Ralph asked again more insistent this time.

"She said that you weren't the guardian and that we were to help Harley. She said the bank was acting as guardian for Harley," Laura said. "We don't know what to think."

"Bernice is all roused up!" Ralph said. "She's a lot like her mother, my wife Irma. I'm supposed to be the guardian, but she's causing a fuss about it."

"What should we do?" Polly asked.

"I'm going to see my attorney again. To put it plainly, she's trying to say that I'm not in my right mind. Can you imagine that! After all I've done for that girl," Ralph said, now wiping his eyes with his handkerchief. "She went to the best schools and always had the best of everything. I don't understand it. I was never as close to her as her mother. But I did the best for her that I could."

Harley stood beside Ralph not speaking although nodding as he followed the conversation, and stretched an arm about Ralph's shoulder giving him a hug. Ralph now took Harley's hand and held it.

"You go along with what she wants for the time being. We'll get this settled," Ralph said.

"Have they settled the investigation about Ethel's death?" Laura asked. "We figured they were through asking Harley questions."

"They're finished with Harley for the time being. Harley told them some things they didn't know." Looking to Harley he added, "You did a good job, Harley," taking his hand and squeezing it. "They say that whetstone was used to strike Ethel's arms and chest. They say she had been attacked before she fell down the stairs. . .probably backed up to the steps before she fell."

"Did Harley hear or see anything? Was he home?" Laura asked.

"We're not supposed to talk about it, but 'yes' he did hear

things. He was home when it happened," Ralph said.

"Me hear. Angry voice yell to Effel. Aunt Effel fall and cry," Harley said. "Go to cellar, see Aunt Effel on floor. Stone by Effel. Take stone hurt Effel."

"It must have been awful for you Harley," Polly said. "No wonder you wanted to stay at our house."

"Maybe we've asked too much," Laura said. "We don't want to cause trouble."

'I'll take the basket to the kitchen. You can return it and the dishes later," Polly said moving on to the small kitchen Ethel had decorated with blue and white gingham curtains.

After goodbyes, they walked the short distance to their own kitchen and the semi-warm tuna casserole. Though neither spoke at the time, each knew it was no longer a question of if Ethel was pushed, but why and by whom?

"I kept thinking about Harley and Quinton as babies," Polly said. "I wanted Ralph to know that I knew. But, didn't think that would be a good idea."

"You're right. We need to be quiet. He probably wanted Wally to keep all that in confidence. I can't imagine how this has affected Ralph. Harley hasn't been here all that long. I'm sure Ralph is still adjusting to the idea. Imagine, twins, and one of them died in the war, and Harley handicapped." Laura said.

"We still don't know how Ralph got all that information. Ethel was so private. I don't believe she would have told him that he was the boys' father. Do you suppose he got in touch with Janette? I doubt if she would be shy about telling him,"

"Then it comes back to what happened to Ethel? Who wanted her out of the way?" Polly asked. "None of this would put her in danger, would it?"

"We don't know the whole story, sister. But I think we're onto something. We're seeing parts, but don't know how they fit together. Don't forget how angry Bernice acted about Ralph being Harley's guardian. Is she protecting her mother's honor, or her inheritance? It seems she blames Ethel, but enough to harm her? I don't know. I'd like to find out," Laura said.

"We shouldn't say anything about this new information to the Sampler Club. I would feel like I was violating a trust," Polly said. "Besides, we don't even know if it's true."

"Do you remember when Nettie told us about what Ethel said about adopting Quinton? She hadn't understood what Ethel meant when she said she should have taken his brother too, or some such thing. Do you remember her saying that?" Laura asked.

"Yes, I vaguely do. I didn't really concentrate on that part. I was so surprised to hear that Quinton had been adopted, I was thinking more on that part. I'll bet she was talking about the other twin. After what happened to Harley, his being injured, Ethel would have felt guilty," Polly said.

"We have to be careful sister," Laura warned. "We can't think we have it all figured out. These are just ideas you know. We're just assuming that is what Ethel was talking about."

"I know, but they sound like they fit, don't they?"

"Yes, but," Laura added, "we still don't know who hurt Ethel."

## CHAPTER TEN

The Peace Lily blossom had opened more fully and a new leaf was starting to unfurl when the Sampler Club met on Thursday. "It's a sign from Ethel," Nettie said. "She wants us to know that she's in a good place. Bless her heart."

"Amen to that," Thelma said, and the others agreed. Each hovered about the lily; touching the smooth green leaves and agreeing that it was doing well out of the direct sunlight, but near the front window of the shop. "It's the time of year when we need to see something alive and blooming," Thelma remarked. "My forsythia is just about ready to open."

"Would you believe, purple crocus and snowdrops are blooming right now beneath my kitchen window? They get the east sun, you know," Vesta added. "It just makes a person smile to see them."

"Did you all see the tulips starting up outside the shop?" Polly added. "We planted extra bulbs last fall. I forget what color they're supposed to be. Do you remember, sister?"

"No, I think maybe it was a mixture of colors. It'll be a nice surprise," Laura answered.

After the initial greetings to each other and Belle, the ladies settled in their usual chairs around the work table. Vesta had adopted a quilted cushion she liked for her back since they last met. "My old bones are getting creaky," she said. "This pillow feels good," she added adjusting it just so.

"How did we do with the extra blocks for Ethel's quilt? Laura asked.

"I've got mine done," Thelma said, taking it from her basket. "I didn't get far with my own, but Ethel's is done."

"That's the way with me," Nettie said placing the block for Ethel's quilt on the table beside Thelma's. "I wanted to do her's first."

Soon they all agreed that they had worked on Ethel's blocks first and were behind with their own as each displayed her 'Ethel block' on the work table. "I think this will be the nicest quilt we have ever made," Thelma added.

"Now I want to hear what's happening." Nettie said, cutting right to the facts of the matter. "You know what I'm talking about."

"I do, Nettie," Laura answered. "I don't want us to get into the habit of gossiping about people. We all admired that Ethel didn't do that, but everything seems so unsettled about her death. The investigation isn't over yet."

"What I want to know is what does Ralph Stillwell have to do with Harley?" Nettie asked. "Is he still staying at Ethel's place?"

"I want to know that too," Vesta said. "His car is parked there all the time."

"We need to make sure we aren't hurting people's reputations when we talk about things," Polly said. "Some things we might think are true really aren't. We can't say for sure we know all the facts. And even if they are facts, will talking about them hurt others?"

"I understand that," Nettie said. "But it seems to be a fact that Ralph Stillwell is living with Harley in Ethel's house. Is that true? And, I don't think that fact is hurting anyone."

"Polly Esther and I took some food to Harley and Ralph

last evening. And I would say, 'yes.' Ralph and Harley are living there," Laura said.

"Has Harley been cleared from any part of Ethel's death?" Nettie asked. "If he hasn't, I want to know."

"From what we understand, Harley was able to tell the police that he heard a loud voice yelling at Ethel the day she died. He heard Ethel fall down the steps and later found her. He also found the whetstone that injured her," Laura went on. "Harley had told the police what Ralph told us, but Ralph said he wasn't supposed to talk about it. We didn't ask more."

"Do you think Harley was telling the truth?" Thelma asked.

"I do," Polly answered.

"Me too," Laura added. "Harley may have his problems, but I don't think he is a liar. I think he is innocent of any wrong doing."

"I would think that too," Thelma added

"I agree. Harley doesn't know about telling lies or making up stories. I think we should have sent him birthday cards," Vesta said.

"We probably should have. Well, it's too late now unless we send belated ones, and that might seem strange to get them late from all of us. We had better just skip that. Who do we think he heard? Did he recognize the voice he heard? Who would do such a thing? Maybe none of us is safe," Thelma said.

"What does Ralph have to do with Harley? I still haven't had my question answered. Does anyone know?" Nettie asked again. "I think Ralph is in this somehow."

"Ladies, we heard some things about Ralph, but I'm not sure we should pass the information on. It may be true and it may not be," Polly said.

"I think we should just be aware that Ralph may be involved. I don't mean in Ethel's death, but that he and Ethel shared some knowledge about Harley," Laura said.

"Was Ethel Harley's real mother?" Nettie asked.

"No, we know that much. Janette, Ethel's sister, was his real mother even though she doesn't act like it," Laura responded.

"Well, tell me this, is Ralph Harley's father?" Nettie asked further.

"Nettie, you have a lot of questions. And we don't know the answers to all of them. You've been reading too many mystery stories," Laura said.

"Well, is he Harley's father?" Vesta also asked.

"It would appear that he may be," Laura finally said. "At least that seems to have been what Ralph told Wally. I think I've said too much."

"Can you imagine how Irma would have taken that? Ralph being Harley's father!" Nettie said. "She wouldn't have wanted anyone to know that. Now would she?"

"It seems she didn't ever know that herself," Polly said. "I think Irma ruled in that house. Can you imagine him telling her such a thing?"

"Ladies, we're getting a little judgmental, and that includes me. I think we need to watch our tongues," Laura cautioned. "We don't even know for sure if Ralph is Harley's father. We can't go in that direction."

"Well, I for one have already gone in that direction," Thelma said. "I thought that when I saw how Ralph treated Harley at Ethel's funeral. Ralph Stillwell wasn't the sort to treat just anyone like he treated Harley. And him getting Harley out of jail and staying with him. What else could be the reason?"

"That still leaves the question. Who hurt Ethel, either on purpose, or accidentally caused her to fall down the cellar steps?" Thelma said.

"You know they always say there's a motive, a reason, why somebody commits a crime. What do you think the motive is in Ethel's case?" Vesta asked.

"Who are the suspects? We don't know, do we?" Thelma inquired.

"I would say 'Irma' if Ralph is Harley's father. Ethel would probably have known if that was true since Janette was her sister. But, Irma's been dead for over a year. Who else would there be?" Vesta continued, "unless it's someone actin' on Irma's behalf."

"I've got to sort this out," Nettie said. "There's a part of the story we don't know, but I intend to find out."

"You know, if someone would hurt Ethel for knowing a secret maybe they would hurt any one of us too if we find out," Polly added. "Remember when Ethel told us that her horoscope said that she should be cautious? I think we should all be cautious about digging into this too much. We should let the police do their work. We might find something we don't really want to find."

"I'm still planning to make my list of suspects and motives," Nettie continued. "Maybe I can give the police some tips."

"I plan to do the same," Vesta added. "We can at least keep our eyes and ears open."

"I'll keep talking to Sue Ellen to see if Homer has told her anything else," Thelma said. "You know my son-in-law is the marshal."

"Not to change the subject, but my birthday is next month," Vesta added. "I don't want anyone to mention my horoscope. I've decided not to read mine anymore. Just in case, you know."

"I'm beginning to feel the same. First Ethel died on her birthday, then, did you notice, Harley was in jail on his," Nettie said. "I don't think your horoscope is supposed to always be bad, but so far it has been."

"Does that mean that we believe it has power over us even if we're afraid to check it out?" Thelma said.

"Oh dear, I didn't think of that," Vesta said. "We're in trouble if we read it, and in trouble if we don't. Is that what you're saying?"

"I don't know. Now I wish we weren't even doing these blocks each month and we're not even half-way through with them," Thelma responded.

"It's down-right scary to think we may have brought this on ourselves," Vesta said.

"I'm sorry," Laura said. "Polly didn't want us to do them, but I insisted. It's my fault. What do you think we should do?"

"I've got an idea," Thelma said. "We could just make six of the blocks and make lap robes or a twin sized quilt instead of a full sized one. How would you feel about that?"

"I've got another idea," said Polly. "Why don't I see if Pastor George could come to our next meeting and talk to us about this zodiac thing. I for one don't think I have the right mind about it all. I've felt guilty from the first day we ordered the patterns. I don't know what to think."

"I'm for that," Nettie said. "I'm beginning to feel strange about these zodiac blocks too. Let's hear what he has to say." Everyone agreed with Polly's idea, depending of course if Pastor George was available.

Thelma added, "So as to not have wasted our time so far, maybe we could just end with six zodiac blocks if Pastor George tells us it's wrong to finish the whole set. We would need six blocks for the twin quilt. We could leave it at that." Thelma said.

"I agree," Laura said. "We can't let fear make us think crazy. After all, we wanted to finish a full sized quilt to give to Harley. But, we could make a twin sized one just as well and it would be faster."

"I hadn't thought about that," Nettie said. "He probably needs a twin sized quilt anyway. Whatever, I'm not going to read my horoscope anymore either, just in case." After their conversation, the ladies worked quietly cutting out the new pieces.

* * *

Pastor George agreed to come during club next Thursday, at least for an hour. It was getting close to Easter and there were other demands on his time. Polly Esther thought it might be good to serve angel food cake while he was there, but Laura said, "no." She thought they should only take time for the conversation, not refreshments. Polly reluctantly agreed. She would have coffee and tea available though.

"I commend you ladies for being concerned about your thoughts and beliefs," Pastor George began. "Miss Polly Esther has filled me in on your dilemma."

"We're so confused, Pastor. We thought maybe you could help us," Nettie said and the others agreed.

"I'm afraid it's my fault," Laura said. "I liked the patterns so much I wanted to do them regardless of what their names were."

"I had a sermon about false gods some months ago if any of you remember," Pastor George went on.

"Yes, I do," Polly said. "I thought you were talking right at us at the time."

"Well, I wasn't. I didn't even know about your quilt patterns and how conflicted you were feeling.

"As I recall, I was speaking about Paul's writings in the book of Acts. He saw that the people of Athens worshipped many gods. They even had an altar to an unknown god. Paul took that opportunity to introduce them to the living God, not one made by the hands of man. He went on to tell them that the gods they made didn't have any power. They would eventually crumble and break. The God Paul spoke of was the creator and sustainer not made by human hands and would live forever."

"But what about the zodiac signs, Pastor," Vesta said. "What about them?"

"Long ago people had many questions about the world around them," Pastor George began. "We still have questions, but we have more answers now than then. It was easy to see the greatness of the sun, moon, stars, mountains, storms and lightning, and even of some powerful people.

"They began to make up stories to answer some of their questions. Stories got passed down and built on through the years until they came to be accepted as true. The zodiac signs are related to some of those stories. They included tales of events and people who were larger than life, who had special powers. Their powers were assigned to the configurations they saw in the stars and other heavenly bodies. At various times of the year they were more evident. There is no real power in the zodiac other than what we give it. They are a part of the superstitions which developed in the ancient world."

"Then we don't need to be afraid of them?" Polly asked.

"Superstitions such as the zodiac draw us away from God. We can come to believe they have magical power over us which hurts our relationship with God. The first commandment says that we shall have no other gods before us. That applies to the signs of the zodiac and what they represent," Pastor George said.

"Then we shouldn't do the patterns?" Vesta asked.

"I didn't say exactly that," Pastor said. "Do you have a black crayon and some masking tape, Miss Polly or Miss Laura?"

"Yes, I can get those for you," Laura Alice said.

"Could you bring me one of your quilting pattern pieces too?"

"Sure," Nettie said, as she opened her pattern folder and handed a piece to Pastor George. "Here's one of mine that we're supposed to work on today. It says Aries right on it."

Taking the masking tape and crayon, Pastor George said, "Can anyone think of a virtue that you relate to your dear friend Ethel?"

"I sure can," Nettie said. "Ethel was patient. She was so patient in helping me learn my singing part in the choir." All agreed that Ethel was patient.

Pastor George took the crayon and printed the word 'patience' on the tape before he tore off that strip and placed it over the 'Aries' word on the pattern. "Now, you're not going to be working on a block titled Aries. You're going to be working on a block titled 'patience.'

"I encourage you to rename each block of your quilt with a virtue that you think applies to Ethel. That will truly make it a memory quilt for her. Will that work?"

"It will work for me," Polly said. "I'm ready for us to do just that."

There were hugs all around and a few tears shed as the ladies began their new assignment by tearing off strips of tape, writing 'patience' on them and affixing them to their patterns.

"I'm sorry I don't have time to stay any longer," Pastor George said. "Are there any other concerns I should be aware of before I go."

"We have a tendency to gossip, Pastor," Laura Alice said, "but we're working on it."

"Be sure to read Romans 1:28-29 and think on what you read there. I hope it helps you understand the seriousness of gossip. I will keep you in my prayers. Good-day, ladies."

After Pastor George had left, Vesta said, "I wonder if Pastor George would consider becoming a member of our quilting group?"

"I doubt that, but we can each thank him again on Sunday for coming. I think he settled our minds about the zodiac sampler. It is now Ethel's Sampler," Polly Esther said.

"Amen to that," Nettie said, after which 'amens' were heard from all.

"I'm curious about that scripture Pastor George said we should read. What did he say?" Vesta asked.

"Romans 1:28-29. I wrote it down on my pattern piece," Nettie said. "Does anyone have a New Testament?"

"I do," Vesta said digging in her purse for the little burgundy colored New Testament she carried. Taking it out, she soon found the place and began to speak.

"Well, it seems to start in the middle of something, but I'll read what it says:

> And just as they did not see fit to acknowledge God any longer, God gave them over to a depraved mind, to do those things which are not proper, being filled with all unrighteousness, greed, malice; full of envy, murder, strife, deceit, malice; they are gossips. . .

There's more, but that's the special part he wanted us to read," Vesta concluded, looking around at the stone-faced quilters.

"I think we've heard enough," Thelma said. "Is it saying that gossips are as bad as murderers?"

"I suppose it's like killing a person's reputation," Polly said. "It sounds serious to me."

"Me too," Laura added. "Who would have thought? I don't remember reading that before."

"Me neither," Thelma said. "I need to think about this more. Do you think it matters if it's something true or not?"

"We all need to think about this more. I for one know that I don't want people talking about some of the things I do even if they are true," Polly said. "We all make mistakes."

"It's being charitable to try to think the best of others," Vesta added. "We don't want to hold a mistake over somebody."

"Sometimes I feel so bad about mistakes I've made," Nettie said. "I sure don't want everybody and their brothers to be talking about them. Remember when. . . no, I won't say what I'm thinking about."

"They say confession is good for the soul, but it may not be good to confess to a gossip. That's what I say," Vesta said. "I'd trust any of you, but I agree, we shouldn't be gossiping about others. It's not good for them, or for us either."

"Amen to that," Laura said. "I learn so much from you ladies."

Before the group broke up for the day, there were hugs and kind words of appreciation for friendship. Outside, Karl beeped his horn three times and the lesson for the day was over.

## CHAPTER ELEVEN

    Easter Sunday, April the thirteenth dawned with calmness, a chill in the air, and no frost. Brilliant hues of red, gold and purple streaked across the eastern sky in Deerfield, Indiana. The full impact wasn't visible from Sisters' Shop because Wally's Barber Shop and Emporium stood in the way. However, both sisters walked north past the shadow of his building to get the full effect. The space between Wally's shop and the bank parking lot offered a spectacular view. Belle walked with the sisters and seemed in awe too as she stood 'woofing' in the sun's direction. "Even Belle knows this is a special day, doesn't she," Laura said and Polly agreed.

    The Easter ham had been picked up yesterday from Cox's Market. The potato salad had been made and was chilling in the refrigerator along with the pickled eggs which had been pickling in the beets and beet juice for four days now. At last turning they were a brilliant red. The yeast rolls were rising covered with a damp cloth on the back of the range, and the jar of home canned green beans was on the counter ready to be opened later. And finally, an orange-pineapple cake had been baked and frosted with a coconut buttercream frosting ready for dessert. Each sister had her specialty in preparing for the feast ahead. They had taken turns being in the shop helping with final sewing projects while the other made good use of her time in the kitchen. Now all was in readiness for the day and their special guests, Harley and Ralph who were coming. They had also been invited to come to church. Wally had been asked to dinner after church as well, but was going to be with his daughter and her family in Trenton.

The church parking lot was filling quickly when the sisters arrived. They spotted Thelma with her daughter, Sue Ellen, son-in-law Marshal Homer Collier, and Skipper, Thelma's grandson, and waved. Marshal Collier greeted the sisters, then told his wife that he and Skipper would wait outside for a while to make sure there were no parking problems. The others went inside.

The pew the sisters usually sat in behind Thelma's family was already filled and the sisters sat two rows back on the inside aisle. The sisters were barely seated when Laura leaned over to Polly. "Do you see who is sitting in our old seats?" and Polly strained her head about to see.

"It's Ralph and Harley! Well, bless them. That makes my day," Polly responded.

"I can smell those lilies clear back here," Laura whispered. "Do you have an extra hankie if I need it? My nose is acting up already," she said, taking a crochet trimmed hankie from her purse.

"Here, take it all ready. You'll need it more than me," Polly replied handing her specially trimmed hankie to her sister.

Vesta started playing the organ and the choir took its place. There was Nettie and the others wearing the gold colored robes the sisters had made for the choir several years ago. "Those robes still look quite nice," Polly whispered to Laura.

"We do nice work," Laura whispered in reply. "Did you happen to see Hazel in her new dress near Ralph?"

"Yes, that collar turned out right nice. I think Pastor George is about to begin," Polly replied.

Pastor George rose from his seat, went to the podium and with his arms extended, said in a clear strong voice, "Alleluia, the Lord is risen! Is risen indeed! Let us all rejoice! Please stand, open your hymnals to page 289 and join together in singing 'Christ the Lord is Risen Today.'" The organ rang out and the vibrant voices of the choir and congregation filled the church with sounds of tumultuous praise. There were smiles on faces and indeed all seemed right with the world except for Laura's runny nose.

All the preparation helped to make Easter a beautiful day. Harley and Ralph were on their best behavior and manners. At Easter dinner with Laura Alice and Polly Esther, Ralph knew to take the hands of those nearest him at the table as Harley led in a prayer of thanks for the day and the meal. The conversation was cheerful with Ralph commenting about the number of people he saw at church that he had known from the bank. Harley too spoke of those he knew from the lumberyard. Everyone enjoyed the ham, potato salad, beets, eggs and especially the orange-pineapple cake which the sisters served with after dinner coffee. Harley and Ralph each had seconds of everything. Harley even offered to help with the dishes later, saying that he helped Aunt Effel, but the sisters insisted that they would get them taken care of quickly later.

"Oh yes," Ralph said before he and Harley went home, "I almost forgot. I'll be right back." With that, he left for his car and came back in a few minutes. "I got one of the lilies from the church. They said we could have one for a contribution of some sort to the church flower fund. I got it for you ladies. You have been so kind." He handed the flowers to Harley who handed it in the direction of the sisters.

Laura Alice immediately took her hanky and held it to her nose, while Polly Esther wiped away a tear as she accepted the flower. "It was so nice of you to think of us." She said admiring the blooming plant. Laura Alice nodded in agreement behind her hanky. "You are special friends."

Easter was over, spring had come and with it calm settled over Deerfield. The strong winds of March were gone. Trees and bushes now unfurled their yellow-green coats and the landscape of April blossomed. Bright red tulips outside Sisters' Sewing Shop were blooming. Polly remembered now that she had switched the multicolored pack for the all red. There were also blue grape hyacinth and white snowdrop making a beautiful offering of spring displayed right at their doorstep. Polly, trowel in hand, was rooting out a few stray dandelions when Wally walked across the street from his shop.

"Those yellow ones look all right to me," he said, "except it's more patriotic without them. Really, it's good to see anything that's bloomin.'"

"I know, but those yellow ones will soon go to seed and spread all over. I don't want to end up with a dandelion patch," Polly answered. "How's your television set doing these days? I see Harley up on the roof real often."

"I can get Dayton when the weather's clear. Mostly it comes and goes. When it don't work right, Harley gets up there and twists the antenna around for me. He's a decent sort of guy, you know. Always wants to help. Him and Ralph are doin' real well together."

"I'm sorry to say we're kind of in the middle of all that. Bernice is expecting me and Laura to buy Harley's groceries, clothes, and pay bills from the trust fund that Ethel set up. Whenever we've tried to find out what he needs, or what bills there are to pay, Ralph says it's all taken care of. We're supposed to report to her at the end of each month. I don't know what will happen when we tell her that we haven't spent anything."

"I hear she's a 'spit fire,'" Wally added. "Ralph says she's like

Irma. Who knows what she'll do. Say, by the way, this primary election is comin' up real soon. Could I give you ladies an 'I Like Ike' sign to put in these flowers? I put one in my window," Wally said pointing across the street.

"I don't know, Wally," Polly said. "We try to stay neutral, for the customers' sake you know. I'll ask sister. Besides, him bein' a general, maybe that means he'd get us into war again."

"You know, it's hard to know what people are thinkin.'" Wally said. "My thinkin' is he'd know how to keep us out of war. He knows how terrible war is.

"A month ago everyone was talkin' about Ethel and what an investigation would show. Now I don't hear much about it. Now they're talkin' about the primary."

"People talk until they've said all they know to say; then, they forget about it. I don't think we've heard the last about Ethel's death. It's just not fresh news anymore. The person that attacked her probably thinks he's got off free. That's what I think," Polly said.

"I think you're right. I have some suspicions, but I don't want to say yet," Wally added. "Let me know if you'd like one of them political signs. I'd best get back to the shop."

"We'll see you Friday evening won't we?" Polly asked.

"Sure will, the good Lord willin' and the creek don't rise," he said, chuckling to himself as he waved and headed back across the street.

Polly had barely settled into her weeding again when a late model blue Buick pulled in front of the shop. She shielded her eyes from the bright sun to see who it was. Out stepped Bernice Hackett, the lady from the bank, Ralph Stillwell's daughter. She walked to the sidewalk then waited looking behind her car. Marshal Collier's official car soon pulled in back of hers and he proceeded to join her. They both walked toward Polly in what would seem to be official business.

"We need to see both you and your sister," Bernice said. Marshal Collier nodded in agreement.

"She's inside," Polly answered. "Did we do something wrong?"

There was no immediate answer as the three went into the shop where Laura Alice was working on the quilt in the frame. "We have company, Sister," Polly said. "Maybe I had better put the 'closed' sign in the window," which she proceeded to do.

Laura slowly got up from the quilting frame and led the guests followed by her sister to the Sampler Club work table and chairs. After they were seated, Marshal Collier spoke. "Ladies, there isn't any need to be afraid. You haven't done anything wrong. Bernice here just wants to let you know what's going on since you two are helping with Harley Flynn."

The sisters visibly relaxed in their chairs, and Polly breathed a sigh of relief. "We haven't spent any money for Harley, honestly there haven't been any expenses. We didn't take any money either," Laura said.

"We're not here to accuse you of anything to do with the money, Miss Laura and Miss Polly," Marshal Collier went on. "Why don't you tell them why we're here," he said turning to Bernice.

"You know my father, Ralph Stillwell, has been staying with Harley," Bernice said. "He has been led to believe that Harley is his son. I didn't want this to get out, but here it is. It can't be left unsaid any longer."

"We heard that might be the case," Polly said. "We promise we won't talk badly about your father, will we sister?"

"Of course not, we wouldn't do that. We promise, marshal," Laura added.

"We're not here about that," Marshal Collier went on, looking somewhat amused by her comments. "Go on Bernice."

"I have reason to believe that my father was told that Harley was his son and that he is being blackmailed," Bernice said. "I know for a fact that my father was never unfaithful to my mother. He couldn't be Harley's father. He's getting senile and will believe anything he's told."

"Bernice wants her father to be examined by a doctor to see if he is in his right mind," the marshal explained. "She wants me to help her take him for a complete physical and psychological examination at the Bluffton Clinic."

"Does he want to go?" Laura asked.

"No, he refuses to go," Bernice said. "However, I'm his Power of Attorney and have the authority to seek medical care if I believe he needs it. Marshal Collier is going to that house where he's staying with Harley and get him. We wanted you to know so you can see to Harley."

"Oh dear, this all sounds dreadful," Polly said.

"Can't there be some other way to have a doctor check him?" Laura asked.

"It's already been arranged. They're expecting my father at the clinic this afternoon. We wanted to get him before Harley gets home from work," Bernice said. "Marshal Collier will help me. Once we get him handcuffed and in the car, he'll be all right."

"Oh no," Polly said as she took her sister's hand. "We're certainly sorry to hear about this."

"It's all that Connelly woman's fault. She's the one who used to live in Trenton. She reminded Dad that her sister used to work at the bank there. All this came up since he was reminded of that. She put ideas in his head."

"I can't believe that Ethel Connelly would tell your father anything that wasn't true. I can't believe she told him that Harley was his son. That just wasn't her way," Laura said.

"You don't know! You don't want to face the facts. My father has been lied to by that woman. Now he's spending money on that Harley person, and even going to change his will. I can't stand by and let him believe her lies."

"I'm sorry you ladies have to be dragged into this," Marshal Collier began. "It won't hurt to have Mr. Stillwell examined. We'll find out if he's all right or not. We'll be going now."

That said, Bernice and Marshal Collier left the shop heading for the house two doors north. Laura Alice and Polly Esther stood mute, their faces frozen with anxiety.

Finally Laura spoke, "We must go on sister. We have a quilt to finish before June. We can't help Ralph even if we want to. We don't know the truth. How does Bernice know that her father was always faithful? Sister, I'm glad we never got married."

"I agree," Polly said as she stooped to pat Belle. "You never cause us any trouble do you?" she said to her. Belle whined a bit and looked at her as if she understood.

Finally, Laura Alice moved to the door and turned the sign to 'open.' She was still standing at the door when Bernice's car followed by the marshal's went past. She could see Ralph seated next to the marshal in his car. What will we say to Harley?

Polly anxiously watched out the shop window for Harley late afternoon. Finally she saw him ride his bicycle past the shop shortly after 4:00 p.m. and told Laura. "Sister, what should we do? Should we go and talk to Harley now or wait?"

"I think we should go now. Ralph's car is still in front of the house. Harley will wonder where he is. I think we both should go," Laura said.

"Oh dear me, I don't know what to say."

"We'll just tell him the truth. Ralph's gone to the doctor to be checked. Bernice, his daughter wanted him to go. We don't have to tell him about the handcuffs or Marshal Collier," Laura said.

"I think that's best," Polly replied.

\* \* \*

Harley was locking his new red bike to the porch railing of his apartment when the sisters arrived. He wore the key to the lock about his neck on brown twine. He saw the visitors and smiled, but continued about his business. While they stood waiting, he took a red farmer's handkerchief from his pocket and wiped down the fenders of the bike. He shook out the dust and put it back in his pocket. Finally, smiling he said, "Raffe got me new bike for my birthday. It red. I keep it clean. He teach me lock it so it won't go way."

"Could we go inside, Harley? We need to talk to you," Laura said.

"I go see Raffe first, so he know home."

"That's what we need to talk to you about, Harley. Ralph isn't here," Laura continued.

"Where Raffe? Where he go?"

"Let's go inside, Harley. We'll talk in the apartment," Laura said.

"Do you want to go in your apartment or the house?" Polly added.

"We go in house. Maybe Raffe come back," Harley said and started around the side of the house for the front door. Arriving, he found the door locked. "I get key," he said moving to the rock where the key was found and proceeded to unlock the door.

Entering, Harley called out, "Raffe, Raffe," then looked puzzled at the silence.

"Let's sit down," Laura said moving to the sofa. Polly sat beside her and Harley in a nearby chair. "You know Bernice from the bank is Ralph's daughter. Do you remember her from when we were at the bank?"

"I know who is. She come here sometime to see Raffe. She

talk loud to him. She talk loud to me."

"Bernice came and got Ralph to take him to the doctor. She wants to know if Ralph is sick. She thinks he might be," Polly said.

"He not sick," Harley said.

"Well, she wants to make sure," Laura said.

"When Raffe be back?" Harley asked.

Polly and Laura exchanged glances, then Laura spoke up. "We don't really know. It might take some time, perhaps several days. We don't really know."

Harley's response to that news didn't take long. He stood, covered his eyes with his hands and commenced the same grievous bawling they had heard before at Ethel's funeral. The sisters sat quietly, not knowing what to say or do while Harley walked about the room continuing his refrain. Finally, taking the dusty handkerchief from his pocket, he blew his nose and wiped his eyes, shook the handkerchief out once more and put it back in his pocket. Now, having regained control of his emotions, he sat down again facing the sisters. "Did she hurt Raffe?" he asked.

"Did who hurt Raffe, I mean Ralph?" Polly asked.

"She hurt Effel," Harley said.

"Did a lady hurt Ethel?" Laura asked.

"Yes, wif stone. I take stone so she not hurt any more," Harley said.

Polly and Laura looked at each other in amazement.

"Who was the lady Harley?" Laura asked.

"I not say," Harley said. "No, I not say."

"Did you hear her say something to your Aunt Ethel?" Laura inquired further.

"Yes, I hear," Harley replied.

"What did she say?" Laura asked as both sisters looked intently at Harley.

"No, I not tell him," Harley said.

"What do you mean?" Polly asked. "Not tell him? Who is 'him'?"

"I not know what you mean," Harley said.

"We don't know either, Harley. Did you talk about this with Marshal Collier?" Laura asked

"No," Harley replied. "He not ask me."

The sisters looked at each other with puzzled expressions. Perhaps knowing the right questions to ask would make the difference.

## CHAPTER TWELVE

Laura Alice and Polly Esther had a house guest for the better part of the week. Harley slept in the guest room on the third floor of the pink Victorian directly above Laura Alice's room on the second floor. He ate breakfast each morning before bicycling to Miller's Lumber, ate a sack lunch at work which the sisters had prepared, and ate his evening meal with the sisters after the shop closed. He helped Miss Polly with the dishes; then went to the house two doors north to check if Ralph had returned. His face reflected his disappointment when Ralph wasn't there.

Laura Alice and Polly Esther gave him the job of taking Belle for her evening walk down to the end of the block and back. The two-some were actually seen running about in the empty lot beside Virgil Shaffer's house, Harley tossing a stick for Belle to fetch. Belle and Harley both returned home in higher spirits than when they started. When Polly tried to take Belle one evening, Belle actually went to Harley and whined tugging at his pants leg. Polly took the hint and gave the leash to Harley. Polly looked at Laura Alice. Would they ever get their dog back?

The Sampler Club ladies came on Thursday with the ladies abuzz about Ralph being taken to Bluffton. Sue Ellen had told Thelma all about that. Homer hadn't really wanted to take

Ralph, handcuffed and all. But what else could he do, according to Thelma.

"Where was Warren while all this was going on?" Vesta wanted to know. "You'd think her husband could have done something. To treat her own father like that, can you believe it?"

"Maybe Warren's afraid of her. You know, Ralph was afraid of Irma. That's what Sue Ellen says," Thelma reported.

"I don't think she should be in charge of the Trust Department at the bank. I don't trust her at all," Nettie added. "I think she's looking out for herself; that's what I think. She doesn't want any of her Daddy's money going to anyone else. That's what I think."

"Ladies, we need to be charitable. We don't know all the facts. Remember that verse about gossip that Pastor George told us to read. Well, I read it again. Right there in Romans gossip is listed with murders and all kinds of terrible things of a depraved mind. Maybe Ralph does need help. We have to consider that," Polly said. "Let's talk about something else."

"I could tell you all about what my horoscope said for today," Nettie went on. "I really didn't intend to read it, then I had it read before I even thought about it. I had even clipped it out. Here it is she said taking the clipping from her pocket, 'No matter what you discuss today, you will be passionately intense about it. Just be aware of this so you know why others react as they do.'"

"That pretty well nails down, what's goin' on. We're goin 'off the deep end. What I want to know is, does any of this have to do with Ethel? I wish I knew," Vesta questioned. "Sampler Club gets more exciting every week."

"Oh dear," said Miss Polly. "What has become of us? Do we want to change our ways or not?"

"We're sorry, Miss Polly and Miss Laura. It's just that everything seems so fearful since Ethel's accident. We're suspicious of everything that happens," Vesta said. "I know I've been afraid. I can't blame it on the quilt. It's just me, and I keep making excuses for myself."

"I'm the one who should be sorry. I can see how people get addicted to things. It happens so quickly. Here I am reading that stupid horoscope when I decided not to," Nettie said. "It isn't right either to thrive on gossip that comes from other's problems. We've got to hold each other accountable. At least that's what I need."

"Remember we're working on the Patience block this month. We could all use an extra dose of that," Thelma said. "You are all like sisters to me and sisters care about each other.

I appreciate it when we can talk truth to each other, but talk it in love. Can we accept that?"

"I agree with that, and 'yes', I can," Nettie said. "None of us should be too proud to accept the help of a sister."

"I agree with that too," Vesta said. "We need to pray for each other every day.

There were hugs all around and Nettie wadded the horoscope paper and threw it away. "I will make good choices in what I read and in what I think about," she said.

The meeting ended decidedly better than the direction in which it had started, yet who knew what next week would bring.

Laura Alice and Polly Esther had decided not to say anything to the ladies of the quilting club about their troubling conversation with Harley. For the first time, they were aware that he knew more than he had said before. It seemed that he was protecting someone, but who? Instead, they would speak to Marshal Collier. Did he know what Harley had heard the day Ethel died? Did Harley really know who the voice belonged to? They weren't sure. "It has to be Bernice, Harley's talking about," Polly said when she was alone with Laura. "What does he mean by 'I not tell him'? Does he know who the lady is that he says he heard?"

"Who else could it be but Bernice? But, why wouldn't he tell if it's her? He says she talks loud to Ralph and to him," Laura added. "We need to let Marshal Collier know what he said. Homer needs to ask Harley some new questions."

The next day, Friday, was a quiet one in the shop. With the full bloom of spring in the air, thoughts of gardening seemed to have won over the urge to sew. Polly managed to bake some salted peanut cookies from a recipe she saw in The Trenton Times while Laura tended the few customers in the shop.

Seven o'clock that evening found both Wally and Harley as guests for game night. Wally tried to teach Harley how to play checkers while Laura Alice and Polly Esther quietly played Scrabble nearby. Finally Wally asked, "Do you ladies have a Chinese checkers board? And marbles?"

"I think we might have the board, but I'm not sure about the marbles. What do you think, sister? Do we still have our marbles?" Polly asked.

Wally laughed. "I've got plenty of marbles in the Emporium if you've lost yours. I'll bring them next week. I think Harley would like that game."

Miss Polly served the salted peanut cookies which were a big hit with the guests. She decided she would keep the recipe. In fact, Wally went home with half a dozen wrapped in newspaper in his sweater pocket, and Harley took a few to his room upstairs to munch on later.

On Saturday morning Wally hurried across the street to announce the good news. Ralph had called long distance from Bluffton Clinic. Warren and Bernice were going to get him on Monday. He was coming home. Wally didn't know the time, or any of the details, just that he was coming home.

Harley, who was eating his breakfast, arose from his chair and actually jumped up and down. "Raffe come home!" he yelled. His mood was contagious and the sisters laughed.

"I go clean house today," Harley said. "I make Raffe proud."

\* \* \*

"Mr. and Mrs. Haskett, I have good news for you concerning your father, Ralph Stillwell," Dr. Wendell was saying in the conference room at the Bluffton Clinic. "While it is commendable you wanting to see that your father had a complete physical and psychological examination, we have found him to be in excellent health. He is well within the range for what is expected for a man of his age. He actually did very well on all his tests," Dr. Wendell was saying as Warren and Bernice listened intently.

"What about the psychological tests?" Bernice probed. "I find it hard to believe his thinking is right."

"He is certainly living in the present. He knows who the President is. He even knows who his congressmen are. He did better than me on that. He can do math very well. He is alert and can use good reasoning to problem solve. We didn't find any problems there. If you're referring to him thinking that he may have fathered a son years ago, he was able to explain why he would think so. Is that what you are referring to?"

"Yes. I know for a fact that he was never unfaithful to my mother," Bernice said with blazing eyes. "He has been coerced by that dead lady into thinking that."

"You're telling me that a dead lady told him that he was the father of a son?" the doctor asked.

"You're twisting it all around. She wasn't dead at the time, but she got what was coming to her," Bernice continued.

"How do you know your father was never intimate with another woman, Mrs. Haskett?"

"My mother would never have allowed it, for one! Another reason is because that woman only wanted to get my father's money. She didn't know I would protect my father. She didn't know who she was dealing with!" Bernice went on, getting louder with each statement and rising from her chair. She was now bending over the table between her and the doctor, shouting in his face. Warren reached out to take her arm. Bernice swatted his hand away. "And don't you try to 'shush' me!" she shouted turning to look at him.

"Mrs. Haskett, I find your comments troubling," Dr. Wendell stated, starting to stand. "I would highly recommend you seek help for your emotions."

"I don't want any recommendations from you. You're a quack, a quack! Do you hear me! Quack, Quack, Quack!" she continued, her face becoming flushed as she spoke.

Doctor Wendell now moved toward the door and stepped from the room. Warren tried to settle his wife putting his arms about her and speaking softly to her. She would not be settled and was actually wrestling with Warren when two attendants entered the room with a restraining jacket. Warren moved aside as the attendants took over.

By 3:30 p.m. Warren and Ralph were headed for Deerfield. Bernice had been sedated and was resting comfortably in the Psychiatric Ward at Bluffton Clinic.

Warren and Ralph traveled quietly at first with just the hum of the motor. They needed to calm themselves following Bernice's episode and admission to the hospital. The visions and sounds of Bernice in full rant still played loud and clear leaving them too exhausted to respond. Finally Ralph began speaking, rather quietly, almost as if he were speaking to himself. Warren didn't say anything, just listened.

He went on about when he and Irma were first married and when he was rising in the bank in Trenton. He talked about Janette Flynn coming to work at the bank and how she had played up to him and seduced him. Ralph went on speaking nonchalantly about the episodes while Warren looked ahead driving down the road gripping the wheel harder at times, completely flabbergasted by what his father-in-law was saying. He told about joining the Army to get away from what he saw as a coming catastrophe; then, finding out while he was gone that Irma was expecting a child. Bernice had been born before he finished his time in the Army and came home. Janette was no longer at the bank by then, and he thought he was 'home free.'

He went on about how years later, after he came to the bank in Deerfield, Ethel Flynn Connelly had opened an account at the bank. Her husband and son had died, and she had her nephew, Harley Flynn living in an apartment in back of her house. She wanted to set up a trust fund for Harley. She said that his mother was her sister, Janette Flynn Marsh. She said that Janette had given birth to twin sons, Harley and Quinton. Ethel and her husband, Cecil, had adopted Quinton and moved to another town. No one there knew that Quinton was adopted. She spoke of the accident in which Janette's other son, Harley, had been injured leaving him with a disability. Janette's husband wouldn't accept Harley and he was placed in a home for handicapped children. Having lost both her husband and Quinton, Ethel had taken Harley to live in her home in his own apartment.

"I could hardly believe my ears at what she was saying," Ralph continued. "Was this the same Janette Flynn I had known at the bank? I asked where Janette had lived and when the boys had been born? My mind was going on and on.

"It all seemed to go together. Harley and Quinton were born less than a month before Bernice was born, actually three weeks. Janette had even lived with Ethel and Cecil in Trenton after the boy's birth, before she married. At the time, her would-be-husband seemed accepting of taking the one boy as his own.

"I knew the boys were mine. I didn't have a doubt but what it was true, but what could I do? Quinton had died in Korea. I had lost one of them in war. That grieved me, but Harley remained."

"Did Ethel know about you and Janette?" Warren finally spoke.

"No, not at first, but I did tell her later. I wanted to get in touch with Janette. I suppose that was foolish, but I wanted to."

"Did you?" Warren asked.

"Not until after Irma died. I never wanted Irma to know. You know how that would have gone."

"I know," Warren said.

"Irma and I only had the one child," Ralph said. "You probably know why."

"Yes," Warren said. "The same reason Bernice and I don't have any children. She doesn't want me to touch her."

The men continued on without any comment for a while. Then Warren spoke, "Did you get in touch with Janette?"

"Yes. Ethel said I shouldn't write directly as it might be a problem for her. Evidently Janette has had some marital problems in the past. She suggested I give letters to her, Ethel, in an envelope and she would put them in a larger one to send on to Janette. They would be addressed in her handwriting and return address. She wasn't trying to create problems, but thought we needed to communicate about Harley.

"Janette assured me that Harley and Quinton were my sons. I never doubted but what that was true. Ethel never told me that," Ralph continued. "Ethel was quite private about Janette and the boys after she told me about her situation and wanting to set up the trust fund for Harley.

"When I look back now, I realize that Irma controlled most

everything about me. I wouldn't wish that on anyone. You're going to have to put a stop to that, son, if you're ever to live in peace. Bernice is very much like her mother."

"Maybe this trip to Bluffton will help change that," Warren said.

"I hope so," Ralph added.

"I got that job for Harley at the lumber yard and pay his salary so they will keep him on. He's smart you know, not like most others, but he's smart. He's my son, and I owe him some things in life," Ralph continued. It seemed he was on a non-stop mission to tell all the things that had been held within for far too long. "I need to change my will to include Harley, but Bernice won't have any part in that. She thinks I've lost my mind."

"I'm going to ask you a question that I hope you won't take wrong. I'm not blaming anyone of anything, but I need to know something," Warren said slowly and cautiously. "Do you think Bernice had anything to do with Ethel's accident? You know how she feels about her and the things she says. Even today she said that Ethel got what she had coming."

"I've had the same thoughts. I don't want to believe that she did, but I know how she can flair up. She's like her mother, a blow torch at times, yet as cold as ice at others. If she did, it wasn't something she planned to do."

"What about Janette? Was she blackmailing you?" Warren asked.

"No, but she wanted to make sure that I would provide for Harley's future. She wanted that and wasn't afraid to say so," Ralph responded. "She and her husband had disputes about paying for Harley's keep at the home he lived in. She was glad when Ethel took him."

They were nearing Deerfield when Warren asked, "Where does all this leave us now?"

"I don't know how all this will end. But, I hope it means I've gained a son-n-law," Ralph said as Warren parked the car in front of Ethel's old house. "We'll see what tomorrow brings for Bernice."

"I'm sorry about all the trouble you've had, Ralph. I hope the future can be better," Warren said reaching across to offer a hand to Ralph. Ralph firmly clasped the hand of his son-in-law and squeezed it before he opened the door.

Ralph leaned in the car to say, "Thank you for listening. I don't know what is going to happen to Bernice. But I intend to be supportive of her no matter what. She is my daughter."

"And I'm not forgetting that she is my wife. Bernice is high strung, but I will honor my vows. I still care for her and will keep you informed about her condition," Warren said before Ralph closed the car door.

Within seconds of the car door closing, the front door of the house opened and Harley came running out. There was a fond embrace before Ralph turned to wave good-bye to Warren as he drove away.

## CHAPTER THIRTEEN

"Marshal, Harley told us about hearing a voice the day Ethel died," Polly Esther said.

"We don't think he had anything to do with Ethel's accident, but we think he knows things that he hasn't told you." Laura continued as she and Polly sat in their kitchen with Marshal Homer Collier seated across the table with a cup of coffee and a cookie before him.

"He says he heard a voice. We believe him and think he's shielding someone, but we don't know who," Polly added. "He says he took that whetstone so no one else would get hurt. That poor boy has been keeping a lot inside."

"He's not a boy, Miss Polly," Marshal Collier added. "He's a man, and we don't know real well what he might be capable of doing. I've been concerned about you two ladies trying to help him. You're too trusting."

"He's a man, marshal, but his mind is like a boy. And I, for one, think he's afraid, just like we've been. He came over here that night when we found him on the sofa in the library. He was afraid to be alone at his apartment," Laura said.

"What! You mean you actually found him on your sofa one night?"

"Well, yes, but he didn't mean no harm," Laura said. "He was just sleeping there."

"Why didn't you call me?" Collier spoke with emotion. "I'd have got him out of here. He can't go breakin' into a person's home!" Collier said, becoming more intense about what the sisters were saying. "That's breaking and entering. It's against the law."

"We didn't want to get him into trouble," Polly said trying to quiet the marshal. "He didn't hurt anything other than scare us at first before we knew it was him," Polly said. "But we settled down after a spell."

"Has he come in here unannounced like that since that time?"

"Well, no," Laura said. "The next time, when Ralph was in the hospital, we invited him to stay. He was here most of the week then."

"Ladies, you beat all! We need to come to an understanding. It is not your job to take care of Harley! I can't allow it. We need to get his mother here. You can't keep doin' for him. His mother's the one who should be responsible for him since Ethel's gone. Some decisions need to be made about that man, and fast! Whether or not she wants to pay the bills for his upkeep or take care of him is beside the point. It isn't up to you sisters or this town to tend to him. You ladies have taken on more than you need to, more than you should," Marshal Collier said, patting Polly's hand. "It's my job to protect you whether or not you know you need protecting'"

"What about the voice? What do you think about that?" Polly asked disregarding the marshal's worries. "We wanted to talk to you about the voice."

"We've had Harley over to Trenton two times earlier to question him. He won't speak up at all to me or the sheriff. We don't know how able he is to talk. I suppose I could question him again, but it would probably be the same. I'm not even sure he understands what we're asking. He seems to talk more to you than to the sheriff or me. We could probably just go ahead and charge him without too much more to go on," Collier said. "He admits to being there. He found the whetstone. Maybe he used it. We don't know."

"Oh, no, marshal, don't do that!" Polly shouted.

"We don't want you to do that, marshal," Laura said. "He isn't guilty."

"Well, it isn't my job just to do what you ladies want," Marshal Collier said. "If you want him to be questioned again, I would suggest you both be there. Would you be willing to do that?"

Laura Alice and Polly Esther looked at each other, "I suppose we could," Laura finally said and Polly Esther nodded in agreement. "You have to know what questions to ask, that's for sure."

"His mother should be present too," Polly Esther added. "She needs to be in on this and hear what he has to say. He's her son and Ethel was her sister."

"I agree," Laura Alice said. "It would be better if you would ask her to come," Laura said to the marshal. "She seems to take charge when we talk to her. She wouldn't listen to us. Maybe we couldn't even get her to come."

"I'll do that. We need to get to the bottom of this accident, if it was an accident. The thing about it was the injuries. Ethel didn't get those from a fall, and the blood on the whetstone was hers. The cuts on her arms and chest were definitely caused by that. Harley's blood wasn't on it. Sheriff Rhodes thinks it was just a case of an elderly woman falling down the cellar steps and somehow hurting herself with a whetstone. He doesn't think there's anything else to investigate, but I don't think that explains her injuries. She didn't give them to herself.

Sheriff Rhodes has other things he thinks are more pressing, so he just doesn't do anything about this case," Collier said. "Another thing, it's over here in Deerfield. He says nothing ever happens in Deerfield."

"All right, I'll arrange for a meeting, but that is all I can do at this point. I'll let you know when and where."

"I suggest you ask Ralph Stillwell to be there too," Polly Esther added.

"I agree," said Laura Alice.

"What is Ralph Stillwell's involvement in this anyway?" the marshal asked.

"Maybe that will come out in the meeting," Laura said. "He's definitely involved. We're not completely certain how."

\* \* \*

"Ralph told Wally at the barber shop, and Wally told my Karl, when he was in the shop watching that television, that Bernice is in the ward, you know for mental problems, at Bluffton," Vesta was telling the Sampler Club on Thursday. "She pulled one of her snits when she and Warren went to get Ralph. Can you imagine that, right there at the Bluffton Clinic!"

"Those doctors at Bluffton won't put up with that. They'll put a stop to it in a hurry. I wonder how Ralph's takin' it, and Warren too for that matter?" Nettie asked.

"I say it was a good thing that she put on a show up there. Now maybe she'll get some help. Irma got away with it all those years, poor Ralph. She'd put up a snit, and Ralph would jump," Thelma went on. "He put up with her. We could've told him she needed help."

"I wonder who's in charge of the Trust Department now?" Nettie questioned.

"How are Ethel's blocks coming along ladies?" Polly asked trying to change the subject. "This is our last week for Patience. What will be the next virtue for Ethel?"

"I'll be ready for another block," Vesta said and held up

the nearly completed block she was working on. That led to a show and tell for all.

"Does anyone have a virtue in mind?" Polly asked. "What do you think it should be?"

"I've got an idea, but there's another thing we have to decide. Not everything that has happened is bad and I think we should go ahead with the full sized quilt," Nettie said.

"I agree with Nettie," Thelma added. "We should go ahead and finish all twelve blocks for ours and Ethel's quilt. After all, we want to do this right, and if we're renaming the blocks after Ethel's virtues, we can do that."

"That's right, and I've got another idea," Vesta said. "I think we should embroidery the names we have given to each of the blocks right down at the bottom of each block. That would help us remember Ethel even more."

"Then do we all agree to go ahead and finish the twelve blocks for our own quilts as well as the twelve for Ethel's quilt?" Laura asked.

"I say we finish all twelve," Nettie said.

"I agree," said Thelma and Polly as well.

"I think the next virtue should be 'joy.' Ethel had bad things happen to her like the loss of her husband and son, but she was a joyful person. She never asked for sympathy, in spite of her own troubles. She would want us to remember her with joy," Polly said.

"Pastor George stopped by yesterday while I was practicing the organ at church," Vesta went on. "He just sat for a while and listened. Then he asked about how our group was getting along. He's praying for us. He said the Lord gives us freedom to make our own choices every day. We are not controlled by the stars, the moon, or any other object on the earth or in the sky. He said the good Lord gives us wisdom to make good choices if we ask for it. I agree with that. Nothing in the stars is deciding what will happen to us."

"Amen to that!" Nettie said. "I had been letting that horoscope mean more to me than I should have. I can choose each day what I will do. That goes for my diet too. Nobody puts that extra food in my mouth, but me. I might as well confess that I want to lose some pounds. That's what my doctor says too. My blood pressure has been creepin' up. Sometimes it seems like I'm in a power struggle with myself."

"Nettie, I have never known you to be in power struggles with anyone else, just maybe with yourself," Polly said. "Remember what the Apostle Paul wrote about the good that he wanted to do, but did not; and the evil that he didn't want to do, that he did. I think that's in Romans."

"Yes, I can understand that. I am like that too. I can't do it alone," Nettie said.

"Neither can any of us," Vesta added. "We have to ask for help from the Lord, and our friends too."

"If we don't finish this quilt, it's like saying that we're afraid of it. Like we think it has some power over us," Vesta continued. "We need to claim the power over things in our life that the good Lord wants us to have."

"I agree with that. We can make the choice on our own of what quilt we will make. We don't have to be afraid," Polly said. "I've been afraid from the beginning. I was letting the zodiac control me."

"Do we feel all right about finishing it now?" Laura asked.

Everyone said they did since they had chosen to rename the blocks. The ladies continued with their handwork while Polly went to get the salted peanut cookies and lemonade she had made for refreshments. Nettie asked if she could just have a few peanuts instead of having them in the cookies. Polly gave her a hug and said, "Yes, and I'm glad you made the choice to ask.

Wally came across the street while the ladies were taking their break, just in time for him to have a cookie or two and lemonade. He had more 'I Like Ike' signs for all to put in their yards. "That Republican Convention is just a little over a month away in Chicago. Ike says he'll end that war in Korea if he's elected President. I've been hearin' all about it on the television. We've got to get him nominated. We're lucky we've got such a man." Each of the ladies took a sign.

Marshal Collier stopped by the shop early on Friday to say that he had contacted Janette Marsh about coming for a meeting concerning Harley. She hadn't wanted to come, yet finally gave in when the marshal insisted. The meeting would be next Monday at Ethel's old house. "That was where the accident happened, perhaps it would make it easier for Harley to remember exactly what he had seen or heard the day Ethel died," the marshal said.

In addition to Harley, the sisters, Janette and himself, Marshal Collier had asked Ralph to be there. Ralph was living at Ethel's now and had been caring for Harley since he paid the bail for Harley to be released from jail. Whatever the connection, he was an interested party. The investigation had been going nowhere with Sheriff Rhodes not convinced Ethel's death was anything but an accident. At least Marshal Collier was willing to give it another try to see if Harley could add anything more.

Wally came over on Friday evening as usual. The sisters mostly listened while he told them more than they cared to know about the upcoming political conventions in Chicago. "They're both gonna be at that Ampitheatre. Can you imagine that, first the Republicans on July 7th, then the Democrats beginning on the 21st of the same month. Old Harry says he won't run any more. He could you know, but he's had enough of it. That Stevenson fella is smart, but he's had mostly book learnin'. Ike's been in the real world. He's a leader. I think those two are what it's gonna boil down to."

"Wally, did you see if you have any marbles in the Emporium?" Polly asked. "Harley's not here this week, but we need to get ready."

"I forgot to look," Wally said. "I've been too busy electioneering for Ike."

The threesome finally settled on playing Rook. They hadn't been playing for long when Wally inquired, "Do you have any more of those salted peanut cookies you had for the quilting ladies yesterday?"

"Wally, I saved some just for you," Miss Polly replied. She left for the kitchen to return with a plate of cookies and glasses of lemonade for all on a tray. Wally smiled and reached for a cookie.

"I sure like these cookies and our Friday night game nights," he said. "We just need to find us another regular. I'm workin' on it."

"What do you mean by that?" Laura Alice asked.

"That's for you to figure out," he responded. "Let's play another hand."

Finally, the cookies had been eaten, the lemonade glasses were empty, the rumpled napkins on three sides of the card table and the Rook cards in a stack. Miss Polly Esther and Miss Laura Alice had seen Wally to the door after a pleasant Friday evening. It had seemed more like the Fridays of the past before the tragedy of Ethel's death.

"I think Marshal Collier is finally taking charge of this investigation," Laura said to Polly after Wally had left. "If the sheriff won't do anything, then I'm glad Homer will. We've all waited around long enough for some action.

"You know, there are two people who just don't set right

with me in this whole thing. Bernice is one. She's a bitter person and she's head strong, but I can't quite believe she attacked Ethel. Harley would surely say if he heard her," Polly said.

"Who would Harley want to protect?" Laura asked.

"He would want to protect Ralph, that's for sure," Polly replied. "But Ralph doesn't seem to have a motive. I think he liked Ethel. Ralph isn't a hot head anyway. I can't see him attacking her."

"There's some little piece we're not seeing. Maybe it will come clear at the meeting on Monday. Getting everyone there will help. If Harley feels comfortable enough, he might tell what he knows. It will help if Ralph is there too," Laura said.

"It should have been done months ago. Thelma said Homer might run for sheriff someday. If he settles all this about Ethel, I'd vote for him. I surely would," Polly Esther added. "And he's such a gentleman too. Have you noticed that?"

"I have. I think he cares about people, but he won't take any guff from them either. I like that about him. That's what we need in a sheriff."

"Let's clean up this mess and get to bed. I want to work on that quilt tomorrow."

"I'm on it sister," Polly said as she started gathering napkins and empty glasses from the table. "We can wash these things with the breakfast dishes."

"I'll take Belle out," Laura said. "Good night sister."

It was an overcast spring night with heavy clouds moving swiftly across the full moon leaving the night blotched in shadows. WOWO had forecast rain before morning. Belle sniffed the air, and walked about a bit before she found the perfect spot for her business. Then as if she heard or smelled something, she barked, growled, and started to run as if in pursuit. "What's the matter, girl?" Laura questioned as she held tight to the leash. "Did you smell a cat, or a squirrel maybe? It'll be all right. Let's go in now. You're all right."

Laura continued to pull Belle's leash to keep her from running to the north. As they approached the house, she actually had to take a hold of the leather collar about her neck and lead her into the house. Once inside, Laura knelt beside her pet as she unhooked the leash and stroked the ruffled fur on the back of Belle's neck. "I've never seen you so upset, little lady. I wish you could tell me what you saw. We're in the house now, girl. It's OK," Laura said, after giving Belle a dog biscuit. Belle licked her hand, whined, and moved on to her bed under the table in the kitchen.

Laura looked once more out the kitchen door window, turned out the outside light, then the kitchen light, and went up the back steps to her room on the second floor. She felt uneasy about what had been so bothersome to Belle.

## CHAPTER FOURTEEN

Outside, in back of the B.P.O.E. building beneath the overhang toward the parking lot a silent figure sat huddled on a bench. She rubbed her bare arms from time to time to warm herself in the damp, coolness of the night air. It didn't help much, but she was intent on her mission and didn't seek shelter. She sat watching the house to the north, Ethel's house. The light had been shining through the apartment door window since she arrived nearly an hour earlier. Was the door unlocked? She was counting on it being so, and knew it often was.

Finally the lights went out, both in the house just south, the sisters' house, as well as the house where Harley lived. The figure waited a while, then crept slowly to the door and finally, boldly took a hold of the knob. It moved. It was unlocked. She didn't push it open, but waited longer gathering her thoughts as she moved back to the overhang at the parking lot.

Large and medium sized rocks which had been painted white lined the space between the parking lot and the lawn. The rocks were clearly visible nearly glowing in the darkness. No one would dare drive over them to invade the Elks lawn.

The figure moved from rock to rock trying to see which could be easily lifted, yet not too small to accomplish her goal. Finally, she chose the best to meet her needs and began to carry it with difficulty from the lot to the apartment next door.

She stopped and put the rock down momentarily to adjust the scrubs she wore. The pants were far too large. She kept tripping as her feet caught in the overhanging legs. She pulled at the tie at her waist fastening it tighter to keep them in place and rolled up the pants legs.

The scrubs, which were actually blue, looked darker in the moonlight. They were stamped with Bluffton Clinic on the back of the top and on the seat of the pants, but it wasn't readable in the darkness. Her feet were clad only in cloth slippers from the hospital making it difficult for her to walk in a natural way on the gravel. Walking on the grass wasn't much easier, it being cold and wet, actually soggy. Each step brought pain to her feet which seemed to penetrate to the bone through each foot rising nearly to the knees. She tried to walk on the sides of her feet which helped somewhat.

Maybe they hadn't even missed her at the hospital. She only pretended to take the pill the nurse brought in. She was smarter than them all anyway. So far, it had worked. Once outside the hospital, she moved from car to car in the parking lot until she found one with the key in place. *Stupid owner,* she thought. It was actually easy to drive away. She had driven without incident to Deerfield, parked in the alley behind Wally's shop and walked across the street to the parking lot after it was completely dark, except when the moon showed through the clouds.

Her mind continued to race with the venom she couldn't control. Let those goody-goody sisters try to solve this one. . . their precious Harley. . .that know-nothing marshal won't begin to know what to do. . .I won't let them take what is mine from me. . .I'll protect Daddy.

What would she do after she had completed her task? She didn't know for sure, but she would probably just drive back to

Bluffton and get into bed. No one would know she had been missing. She wouldn't be a suspect; after all, she was in the hospital.

The clouds thickened further after midnight and it began to rain before sunrise on Saturday morning. It cleared somewhat for a while; then more dark clouds moved in bringing more rain. It was dreary, a good day to stay inside. Wally Newton was taking some trash to the container in the alley behind his shop when he noticed the car. Usually the alley was clear. Why would anyone park in that alley? He checked an hour later, then after another. This was a puzzler. A Willys? Who in town owned a Willys?

"Marshal Collier, this is Wally Newton. I'd like to report a car parked in the alley in back of my shop. No, I don't know who it belongs to. It's been there all morning as far as I know. I can't see any registration on it. It's a two-door tan Willys. It's locked. The license looks like it's from out of the county. Maybe you'd come over and take a look at it."

"What's the matter now, Wally," Ralph said as he came into the barber shop to have some coffee with Wally on this Saturday morning. "You're calling the marshal?"

"Well, yes, it's the strangest thing. There's a tan car parked behind the shop. It may have been there all night for all I know. At least it's been there all morning until now. I've never seen that car around town. Come take a look and see if it looks familiar to you." At that both men went to Wally's back door to look at the car in his alley.

"I've not seen that before. I'd never buy a Willys. I don't like the looks of them," Ralph said. "The front looks like the back."

Just then, Marshal Collier's car pulled in front of the Willys and the marshal got out. "Is this the car you called about?" the marshal asked.

"One and the same," Wally answered.

"I think it may be the car I received a notice about. A car was stolen late yesterday evening from the Bluffton Clinic. It seems a young fella visiting a patient went to get in his car after visiting hours, and his car was gone. Says he left his keys in it. Can you imagine that? That's like asking somebody to take it. Then the law's supposed to find it."

"It takes all kinds, I guess," Wally said. "Maybe he'll be lucky this time and get it back."

"I'll look into it, Wally. Thanks for calling me," Collier said before addressing Ralph.

"Ralph, I'm glad you're here. There's something else I need to talk to you about. Can we get in my car?" Marshal Collier asked.

"Sure Marshal. I suppose it has to do with my getting Harley last evening. I'm still thinking about all that Harley has had to go through. I'm trying to make it up to him," Ralph said as he got into the marshal's car.

They were seated inside as Marshal Collier drew a deep breath before he looked at Ralph. "I hate to tell you this, Ralph, but Bernice is missing from the hospital."

"Missing? How can that be? Was she kidnapped or something? What happened to her?"

"We'd like to know. The hospital said the nurse had taken her medication in at about 7:00 p.m. last evening. It was a sedative to help her relax for the night. The nurse thought she had taken it, but evidently she didn't. When the nurse went in to check on her about an hour later, Bernice was gone and the pill was still in the cup on her night stand. They also said that a car from the visitors' parking lot had been taken at about the same time. They didn't know if the two were connected or not. The car was a tan Willys. It sounds like it could be this car that has turned up here. At least it's the same color and make. I'll have to check on the license to be sure. Do you have any idea where Bernice might be?"

"Why wasn't I notified before now?" an indignant Ralph was asking.

"I was honoring a request made by Warren. He thought you were going through enough with all this about Harley. He thought she would surely show up before now."

Ralph sat with his head in his hands. Finally he looked up. "You'd think an only child would be happy to find out she has a brother, but that's not the way it's been. Bernice has been all fired up about me adopting Harley, acknowledging him as my son. She doesn't want any part of it. She tried to get me declared out of my mind. I don't know where she'd be. I wonder what she's up to now?"

"It would appear that she's somewhere in Deerfield if she's the one who took that car." Collier paused as if collecting his thoughts. "I'll take you home. We can start the search right there. We can stop at the bank and let Warren know that the car may have been found."

"Why would she take a car? I don't understand any of this," Ralph said.

Marshal Homer Collier and Ralph stopped by the bank to talk to Warren who then joined them in the marshal's car. "We'll stop by your house first Warren to see if there is any trace of her," the marshal said.

At Ralph's old house where Warren and Bernice now lived, the marshal walked around outside of the building while Warren and Ralph searched inside. Nothing seemed out of place or disturbed in any way, not even footprints where they might have been found. "Let's get back in the car and go to Ethel's house where you and Harley have been staying," the marshal said.

When they arrived, the marshal indicated that once again he would walk around the house and check to see if any basement windows had been disturbed. Warren and Ralph would check inside and in the basement. It wasn't long until Marshal Collier ran toward the house from the back yard yelling, "I've found her. Come quick!"

When Warren and Ralph reached the back yard, they saw the marshal bent over a body clothed in blue hospital scrubs lying prostrate on the ground. It was Bernice with her arms still extended as if clutching the large white rock her forehead rested on.

"Is she alive?" Warren yelled now also kneeling beside Bernice. Ralph knelt beside his daughter, an arm extended over her, his head bowed near her, he began to cry.

The marshal held his fingers to the side of her neck to check for a pulse. "There's a faint heartbeat," he said looking at the anxious men. "We've got to get her to help. I'll call for an ambulance. She must have been out here all night."

"It'll take too long for an ambulance to get here. I'll take her in my car," Warren quickly answered.

"It may hurt her more if we move her," Marshal Collier replied.

"We'll have to take the chance," Warren said.

"Yes, we have to take her now," Ralph repeated.

"My car's here," the marshal said. "We can take her in it if that's what you want."

"We need to get her back to Bluffton," Warren said. "You can drive faster than me since you've got a marshal's car. Let's get started."

The marshal backed his car onto the parking lot of the B.P.O.E. then he and Warren, as carefully as possible, lifted Bernice onto the reclined front seat of the car. "I don't have room for both of you to go with me," the marshal said when the unconscious Bernice had been loaded and a blanket from the marshal's car placed over her body.

"We can follow in my Studebaker," Ralph said. "It's right in front. Warren, would you drive? I'm too upset." With that said, the threesome set off for Bluffton with a hope and prayer that they would arrive safely with a still living Bernice.

"Sister, look at this!" Laura exclaimed Monday morning as she rushed with the paper to the kitchen. "We didn't know anything about this. Read this" she said pointing to an article titled SEARCH ENDED. "Read it out loud."

> DEERFIELD, Ind. The search ended Saturday morning for Mrs. Bernice Haskett who was reported missing from Bluffton Clinic on Friday evening. Mrs. Haskett is reported to be in critical condition following a fall which injured her head.
>
> Charges of auto theft have also been filed against Mrs. Haskett in a strange set of circumstances. Mrs. Haskett is back again at the Bluffton Clinic, now under tight security.

"What on earth is that all about?" Polly said after she had finished the oral reading.

"I'm afraid to ask Ralph. He must be crushed. Imagine, Bernice stealing a car. Is that what is says? I can hardly believe that. Why would she do that? And hit her head in a fall. Did she fall in the hospital? That woman needs serious help."

"It sounds very serious, critical condition, tight security. She surely needs our prayers, and Ralph does too. No one said a thing at church yesterday. Sue Ellen must not have told Thelma about it."

"Remember there was an unspoken prayer request. I think Sue Ellen made that," Laura said. "We need to take those serious, you know."

"At least we know there's a real need. We've had enough gossip to deal with, we don't need more. This evening we have that meeting about Harley, and it's still raining."

The meeting with Marshal Collier with the sisters, Janette Marsh, Harley, and Ralph was to be at 5:30 p.m. in Ethel's house. In setting the time Marshal Collier was considering the ladies business hours, Harley's work hours, and time for Janette to travel from her home in Ohio, never mind his quitting time. Besides, it seemed he didn't really have a quitting time. He was on call all day and all night seven days a week.

The sisters saw Harley riding his bicycle past the shop in a misty downpour shortly after 4:30 p.m. They closed the shop at 5:00, as usual, took care of the receipts, and straightened the shop for tomorrow before they left for the meeting. They both shared an anxiety about this meeting. "Sister, I just feel that something will come out of this get together. I don't know what, but I just feel it," Laura said.

"I wish I shared your hope. It seems like a lot hinges on this meeting. We have to protect Harley. It sounds like the marshal wants us to quit botherin' him and show some evidence of there bein' a crime. That's what I'm thinking," Polly said.

"I think you're right. Keep your eyes and ears open. Let's face it, it may be up to us or the law will just say the whole thing is closed. That's what the sheriff wants to say," Laura said as they left for Ethel's house.

Ralph and Harley were there when they arrived. Harley had brought his bicycle up onto the porch and was wiping off the rain and shining it. Ralph stood in the doorway watching him.

In the living room the sisters asked Ralph how Bernice was getting along. "She's still unconscious," he said, "but the doctors are hopeful." They didn't ask further. Ralph appeared cheerless and tired, not attentive to his guests. The sisters took seats in the living room while Ralph walked about nervously preoccupied. He finally went to the porch to ask Harley to come into the house and put on a dry shirt.

Janette Marsh came about ten minutes late. She exchanged a sullen greeting with the others and was seated. It was difficult to exchange small talk in the group. The sisters asked if it was raining in Ohio, then the conversation dried up. Janette fidgeted on Ethel's sofa for a while, then took out a pack of cigarettes and a lighter. She was in the act of lighting up when Ralph spoke up to say, "I don't like to smell tobacco smoke, Janette."

"So, who made you the boss in my sister's house," she said and continued to light up.

"I don't like it either," Laura said.

"Well, I'll go outside to smoke," she replied, "blowing a cloud of smoke back into the room as she stood."

Just then, Marshal Collier came into the room. Harley who had been putting on a dry shirt until now arrived through the kitchen. He spotted his mother, and lifted a hand to wave briefly, but sat in a chair beside Ralph.

"I'm sorry I'm late," the marshal said. "It's been a busy day, and I had to check on something.

"I noticed the car outside with the Ohio plates. I'm assuming it belongs to Janette Marsh. That would be you," he said turning toward Janette who was still standing, cigarette in hand.

"Yes, it's mine," Janette said. "Is there something wrong? Did somebody hit me or something?"

"No," Marshal Collier answered. "It's parked going the

wrong direction. You crossed over to the other side of the street to park your car in front of this house."

"So what? It's not like I caused an accident."

"No, you didn't, but it's parked illegally. I was checking my book. I've written some other tickets for that same car parked illegally in front of this house," Collier continued.

"Let's sit down, Janette," Collier said pointing to a chair near the fireplace. He sat in another chair on the other side of the fireplace from Janette. The front window was to her left.

"Hi Momma," Harley finally said.

"Hello Harley," Janette said looking at her son seated next to Ralph on a straight backed chair.

"Mrs. Marsh, as I was saying, I have written several other tickets for illegal parking for that same car. There has been no response to the other three. The first ticket I have a record for was on December 20th, at 1:00 p.m. of last year, 1951, the next was at noon on March 11th of this year, then several days after that on March 15th in the morning, now today."

"All right, what do I have to do now? Say I'm sorry?" Janette answered taking another drag on her cigarette and blowing the smoke in Ralph's direction away from the marshal.

"I notice one of those dates is March 11th," the Marshal said.

"So what? I said I was sorry," Janette retorted.

"I know what that date is," Laura announced.

"I know too," the marshal said looking at Janette. "It was the date of your sister's accident, right here in this house. It puts you at the scene of the accident on that date. The time on the ticket is about an hour before I was summoned to come here by your son Harley."

Janette looked at Harley. "What did you tell him?" she demanded angrily.

Harley's eyes widened and his arm clasped onto Ralph's sitting next to him. "I not tell him! I not tell him!" he yelled out as he started to cry. "I not tell him, Momma!"

Janette doused her cigarette in the flowerpot holding the dried up geranium on the table near her and hung her head low over her crossed legs and arms.

"What didn't you tell, Harley? Was it that you heard your mother's voice the day your Aunt Ethel died?" Laura asked gently.

Janette bolted out of her seat, looking with narrowed eyes at Harley. Laura, still seated, continued to hold eye contact with Harley.

"Yes, I hear Momma's voice, but I not tell," he said looking at Laura. "I take stone so Momma not hurt any more."

"Do you want to tell us about that day, Janette?" Marshal Collier asked.

Janette was now wiping her eyes and her nose with the back of her hand. "I didn't mean to hurt her," she said beginning to sob. "She was my sister. She had always helped me. It was an accident."

"What happened?" Collier asked.

"She said I had to tell Ralph something. I didn't want to. I wasn't going to, but she said I had to, or she would tell. It made me so angry. I wasn't going to tell him anything I didn't want to," she said, her voice rising. "Why should I tell him when everything was going good?" she said, now looking at Ralph, then at the marshal.

"Was it about Harley's father?" Laura asked.

"Yes," Janette said looking at Harley, then Ralph, her eye make-up beginning to run down her face.

"Perhaps there needs to be a blood test. Is that in order?" Collier questioned.

Harley looked confused. Ralph gripped Harley's hand in his.

"I don't think there needs to be a test," Ralph said before

pausing and looking down. "Sometimes tests are wrong," he finally said before looking at Harley. "I admit that I am Harley's father. I don't need a test to tell me that."

"But Ralph," Janette spoke up, now looking directly at Ralph. "That's not what Ethel wanted me to tell you."

"I can guess what she wanted you to tell me. It doesn't matter. I plan to adopt Harley. He is my son." Ralph continued, now taking his handkerchief from a pocket, he wiped his eyes and nose.

"Janette, I am taking you to Trenton to see the Sheriff. You will need to make a statement about the events of March 11th here in Deerfield related to your sister's death," Collier said.

"Don't handcuff me, marshal," Janette said. "I'll go. I don't want my son to remember seeing me in handcuffs."

"That's the least of what he will remember about you, madam," Collier said taking his cuffs from his belt.

## CHAPTER 15

On Wednesday The Trenton Times carried another story from Deerfield on the front page in bold letters, no less. Neither of the recent articles from Deerfield were especially what the citizens of that fair town liked to present to the world, but there they were. At least they spoke well of Marshal Homer Collier. The current caption read, SISTER CHARGED along with an unflattering photograph of the handcuffed Janette Flynn Marsh with mascara stained eyes and cheeks being led into the country jail by Deerfield Marshal, Homer Collier. Polly Esther picked up the paper from the front steps looking at the picture on her way through the shop once she saw the caption. The article read:

> DEERFIELD, Ind. Janette Flynn Marsh, from Springfield, Ohio, has been charged with Manslaughter in the death of her sister, Ethel Flynn Connelly. Mrs. Connelly died on March 11th, 1952 from a fall down her cellar stairs. An investigation followed due to injuries which were inconsistent with a fall. Deerfield Marshall Homer Collier followed leads which led to Mrs. Marsh's arrest. Mrs. Marsh stated that she became enraged with her sister over family matters and attacked her with a whetstone blade causing Mrs. Connelly

to fall. Mrs. Marsh indicated that her anger got out of hand and that it was not her intention to cause her sister to fall. Mrs. Marsh is being held in the Trenton County Jail and has been advised by her attorney to make no further statements about the event before her trial.

Polly Esther proceeded to the library to read the article to Laura Alice who was lying on the sofa with dampened tea bags over her eyes. "I could show you Janette's picture if you like, but you'd have to take those bags from your eyes," Polly said. "Her hair wasn't all in place, and her make-up doesn't look perfect. Her dress looks rumpled, and I'll bet she may have broken a nail or two." Laura Alice made no reply. "Are your eyes still burning so?" Polly inquired.

"My eyes are feeling better, thank you, and 'no,' I don't want to see the picture. I've seen all I want to see of that woman. Through closed eyes, I'm still seeing her face from Monday. I remember how she looked at Harley through those half-closed eyes and puckered up mouth when he said that he hadn't told on her. He still wanted to protect his mother and to have her approval. Then, she was completely dumbstruck when Ralph said, 'I don't need a blood test. Tests are sometimes wrong.' She couldn't believe it. All the conniving to convince Ralph that Harley was his son, when Ralph wanted him to be his son even if he wasn't."

"My estimation of Ralph went way up when he said that," Polly said. "He wanted Harley to be his son no matter what the blood tests would tell. Now that's what love is about. Irma didn't know what a catch she had.

"I was so proud of you too, sister, how you spoke up to ask the right questions. I was sure the marshal was just going to give her 'fits' for another illegal parking ticket. Then you mentioned about it being the day Ethel died."

"The marshal remembered that too. I just verified it," Laura said.

"You asked Harley if it was his mother he had heard that day. I'm not sure the marshal would have asked him that. You asked so gently, he didn't feel afraid to tell," Polly said. "At least take credit for that."

"I'm pleased that the missing piece has been found. I don't want to take any credit. It's a sad story, but at least we know what happened. And, perhaps Harley will have a better life because the mystery has been solved," Laura replied.

"All that time, Janette scheming and conniving to get Ralph to take Harley off her hands. And to think, Ethel knew her secret from way back when. She knew that Janette had tried to cover her condition when she vamped Ralph in the bank; she was already pregnant. Then, Janette tried to catch him again, years later. It was more than Ethel would tolerate.

"No, Ethel wasn't going to let it pass. She was trying to get Janette to be honest. But, that woman doesn't know the meaning of the word. She didn't have to hurt Ethel, Ralph didn't even care whether Harley was his real son or not. He truly cared about Harley," Polly added.

"The judge that hears this case won't know the half of it. Whatever Janette gets out of this, it won't be enough. I know, it's mean of me to say that," Laura said. "'Be sure your sins will find you out.' Remember when mother used to say that when somebody got caught in something."

"Yes, it was usually me, when she found out something I had done," Polly responded.

"Well, me too," Laura added. "Mother was right. Sometimes it just takes longer than others for it to come out."

"Sister, I can't believe, you got that whole Double-Wedding-Ring quilt done last night, but at what price? You were up all night and strained your eyes. They still look red, and you've got circles under them, dark circles."

"That's probably from the tea bags. They probably stained," Laura said, putting them back on her eyes. "I couldn't sleep anyway knowing this needed to be done. Then, with all that happened how could I sleep? I don't know how you do it."

"I'll going to call Eunice Franks to tell her the quilt is done and she can pick it up. That wedding is next week if I'm not mistaken. We sure had enough interruptions in getting this one done. After that, I'm also going to call that eye doctor in Trenton. You can't keep getting glasses from Wally's Emporium. It's time you have your eyes examined by a real doctor, and get a real pair of glasses!"

"I hear you. There's nothing wrong with my ears, nor my eyes either for that matter. I just overdid it. You know, Harley shouldn't see that paper with the picture of his mother and all."

"I know, but what can we do? We can't collect all the papers in Deerfield. He's bound to hear about it at work, or see it at Wally's. It's a good thing he has Ralph, and that Ralph has him too for that matter," Polly added. "I think things are going to get better for both Harley and Ralph now that certain women in their lives are out of commission for a while. It's too bad about Bernice, but you can figure out what she was trying to do. How will she ever face people in town again? How can she be in the Trust Department, of all places? Sometimes it takes a big embarrassment to humble a person. Maybe Bernice will change for the better after all she's going through. I hope so.

"Say, there's a little ad right here in the Help Wanted column. It reads: wanted part-time cook and housekeeper. Must be neat and clean, and have references. Apply to Ralph Stillwell at Deerfield phone exchange 2410."

"Well, I'll be," Laura Alice said. "I'll bet you anything one of the ladies, or more than one, from the Sampler Club will apply for that."

"I'm sure you're right," Polly Esther replied. "I'm almost tempted to apply myself."

"No you don't, sister. I'm not about to run this shop by myself. We're in this together," Laura Alice said, suddenly sitting up and tossing the tea bags aside. "Besides, you're the best cook. I don't want to eat my own cooking every day."

The Sampler Club met on Thursday, but the mood was anything but usual. Thelma brought the news account with the picture of Janette and her son-in-law on the front page. "I knew he would do it," she repeated in so many different ways. "He'll be the next sheriff of this county, mark my words."

"Thelma, I'll vote for him if he runs," Polly Esther found herself saying. "If it hadn't been for Marshal Homer Collier, this case would not have been solved."

"Amen to that," the others said.

"And you sisters kept pushin' him too, we won't forget that," Nettie said.

"Is he going to run for Sheriff?" Vesta began. "I don't think this is the year to vote for that."

"Well, when it's time, he'll run," Thelma assured her. "I'll tell him you ladies will all vote for him."

"And what do you make of Bernice Haskett? Does anyone know what that's all about? What was she trying to do? Homer was in on that one too," Vesta continued.

"I say she was on her way to bash Harley in the head, that's what I say," Nettie said. "Has Sue Ellen told you anything about that, Thelma?"

"No, but I'll bet she knows plenty," Thelma replied.

"Why else would she be in Ethel's backyard carrying a rock. She was surely carrying it, don't you think?" Nettie reasoned. "What else would have been going on?"

"Ladies, did we come to quilt or to gossip?" Laura Alice questioned when she caught the quilters between breaths. "Justice has been done. We can let Ethel rest in peace. Now, let's decide what to do about this quilt we're making for her."

"I agree," Polly Esther said, and the others said the same.

The six blocks for a twin sized quilt for Harley were done. However, the quilters decided to keep going for the full sized quilt. It was no longer the zodiac sampler, it was now Ethel's sampler. There would be fabric to choose for the additional blocks, the sashing, the borders, and the backing. Laura Alice and Polly Esther had said they would provide fabric for that, but the ladies of the club all decided they would pay for the extra each of them needed for Ethel's sampler. That was only fair.

When all the blocks were done, Vesta would add the sashing. Thelma would do the borders, and Nettie would add the batting and backing. Laura Alice and Polly Esther would baste it all together and put it in the quilting frame. Then, everyone would pull their chairs up to hand quilt their masterpiece for Ethel. After it was quilted, an identification label would be sewn for the back listing all the ladies who had finished Ethel's sampler and the date it was finished. It would then be given to Harley in memory of his Aunt Effel.

The twelve virtues the quilters chose to represent Ethel were: Patience, Joy, Hope, Faithfulness, Love, Kindness, Prudence, Self-Control, Gentleness, Peace, Persistence, and Generosity. The quilt not only represented their friend Ethel, but the journey they had experienced together during the past year. The Case of the Zodiac Sampler was ended. Ethel's Sampler was in progress.

"Make it a big label," Vesta advised. "We have a lot to say." They agreed it would read: 'Ethel's Quilt finished for Harley Flynn by the Sampler Club, 1952.' Then all their names would be added including Ethel's.

"I'm glad we decided to do this. We couldn't leave Ethel's quilt undone," Thelma said.

"We still have a lot of work ahead of us, but it'll be worth it," Vesta said. "It might take another six months."

"What else could we do that is more important?" Nettie added. "I've given up reading my horoscope. Now I have more time to quilt."

"Did anyone besides me notice the Peace Lily is getting another bloom?" Nettie continued. "It likes its place here in the shop. I think it's a sign from Ethel. She's happy with us."

"Well, I'll be, look at that," Thelma said, "pointing to the new light green growth pushing up in the pot. I think you're right." The others positioned themselves to observe.

While they were moving back to their seats, Vesta spoke up, "Say, I almost forgot, Wally told my Karl something yesterday. I just have to pass on," she said. "It's not just gossip. He really said this."

"What now? I hope not something bad," Nettie responded.

"Well, depends on who is hearin' it," Vesta continued. "It seems Warren is feelin' bad that he and Bernice took over Ralph's house and pushed him out, so to speak. And since Bernice is still in the hospital, he's goin' to do somethin' about it. According to Wally, Warren has made Harley an offer on Ethel's old house, where he and Ralph live now. Can you imagine that? Ethel left it to Harley you know."

"Would Ralph move back to his own house?" Thelma asked.

"That's what Wally said. He said Ralph and Harley would move back to Ralph's big house. He said they would have room for a model railroad in the basement, and lots more room to do things they want to," Vesta added. "Warren would move into Ethel's old house as soon as he can and Bernice would join him when she's able."

"Do you suppose that's so? How would Bernice take to that if and when she gets home?" Nettie asked, but no one answered

"Did you hear about Bernice's surgery," Thelma asked.

"I heard that she had it," Nettie said. "How is she doing?"

"Well, Ralph told Wally, and Wally told Karl that she is doing real well. The swelling in her brain is down and her color is getting better. She's still on oxygen, but she seems to be improving," Vesta said.

"Say, another thing. That would mean that Laura Alice and Polly Esther would have new neighbors," Thelma reasoned. "Is that the part you meant might depend on whether it was good news or bad?"

No one said anything for a while, then Polly Esther spoke. "You know, we can always use another quilter in the Sampler Club."

"I agree with that," Laura Alice added.

"There's something else I want to say," Thelma said quietly, not looking directly at anyone. "Did any of you see the ad that Ralph Stillwell put in the paper wanting a part-time cook and housekeeper?"

The ladies looked at each other as if in surprise. "I didn't see it," Vesta said.

"Me neither," said Nettie looking about the group. "When was it in there?"

"Yesterday," Thelma replied. "It was in the same paper as the story about Janette Marsh." She paused; then continued, "I called about it right away. I just gave my name and number, and said I was interested. Ralph called me this morning and wants me to come over to talk to him about the job."

The ladies reacted to the news with excited cheers. Then each got up to give a hug to Thelma, who was overwhelmed with the response. "I haven't gotten the job yet. There may be others he'll talk to. He wants references. I was wondering if somebody here would give me a reference? I haven't worked at a job where you needed a reference for a long time. I think all my old references are dead."

Vesta, Nettie, Laura Alice, and Polly Esther all quickly said they wanted to be Thelma's references. Laura Alice got a blank sheet of her best stationary and wrote a letter of recommendation which the ladies all dictated to her. They each signed and gave their phone numbers.

"When are you supposed to see Ralph?" Laura asked.

"At 3:30 p.m. today," Thelma announced. "Do I look all right?"

"You look wonderful!" each echoed in return.

"And you came to the Sampler Club anyway?" Nettie asked.

"Are you nervous?" Vesta asked.

"I thought about not coming here today, but if I'd stayed home, I would be nervous," Thelma said. "I knew I would be better off here."

There were smiles all around as the ladies finally settled down to do their handwork. Thelma assured them that she wanted to stay until 3:00. "I'll have plenty of time. He said to come to his old house, the one just north of the church."

"I guess he must be moving back there," Polly said.

A quietness and even peace settled over the working ladies. Perhaps they were thinking of all they had been through together in the last few months and joyful for Thelma with her good news. Perhaps they were thinking of how they had been blessed with friendships that had seen them through difficult times and encouragement to forge ahead. There had been changes and it looked as if there would be more. Their friend Ethel was still with each of them as her witness of doing good remained and nurtured each to do the same.

Wally came over on Friday evening and brought Floyd

Blansett with him. Floyd was a bachelor farmer the sisters knew slightly from church. He had been a part of the scenery at church, but nothing beyond that. Wally, as well as Floyd was sporting an "I Like Ike" pin on his lapel. Wally was also carrying some yard signs for his favorite candidate. "I brought these just in case you ladies would want to make them available to your customers. They're free of charge," he said as he placed them on the hall table.

Laura Alice and Polly Esther looked at each other then at Wally, "You're goin' to keep pestering us until we pass out those signs aren't you?" Laura asked.

"I reckon so," Wally said with a smile. "Somebody has to see that the right man gets elected. Floyd here sees things the same way I do."

"What do you say sister, should we take one of those signs for our yard?" Polly asked.

"I reckon we might as well. If somebody comes round with a 'Stevenson' sign we could always put it up too," Laura responded.

"Wally makes a pretty good case for the General," Floyd said. "Not to change the subject, but you ladies have a nice shop here," Floyd added. "I had never been in here before. These quilts hangin' up are real nice. Do you do repair jobs on farmer's work clothes?"

"Yes, we do alterations," Laura Alice replied smiling at Floyd.

"Well, I've come to the right place then," Floyd replied, smiling back. "I've got a bachelor's ton of clothes without buttons, pants that need patches or shortened, broken zippers, or whatever, that I need 'altered' so to speak  It's all been pilin' up for quite a while."

"You and Wally come right on into the library," Laura offered. "We can have seats in the library, decide what we want to play tonight and discuss your alteration needs, Floyd. Polly made some rhubarb cobbler for dessert later on. Those last rains really brought on the rhubarb."

"A little rain never hurts the rhubarb," Floyd said. "No, siree! I can't remember the last time I've had rhubarb cobbler. I'm in for a real treat. I just know it."

Polly Esther exchanged glances with Laura Alice. Was this Mr. Wonderful? They were both thinking the same, and the other knew it. And to think, Polly Esther hadn't even used her rouge, nor Laura Alice her lavender soap. But then, maybe it wouldn't really matter to Mr. Wonderful after all, not when the sisters could do alterations and make rhubarb cobbler. But, there was only one of him, and two of them. That might be a problem.

## THE END
(Or is it the beginning?)

CPSIA information can be obtained
at www.ICGtesting.com
Printed in the USA
FFOW01n0705130517
35385FF